SPRING
Break
MISTAKE

Also by Allison Gutknecht

Don't Wear Polka-Dot Underwear with White Pants
(And Other Lessons I've Learned)

A Cast Is the Perfect Accessory
(And Other Lessons I've Learned)

Never Wear Red Lipstick on Picture Day
(And Other Lessons I've Learned)

Pizza Is the Best Breakfast
(And Other Lessons I've Learned)

The Bling Queen

SPRING Break MISTAKE

Allison Gutknecht

ALADDIN M!X
New York London Toronto Sydney New Delhi

This book is a work of fiction. Any references to historical events, real people, or real places are used fictitiously. Other names, characters, places, and events are products of the author's imagination, and any resemblance to actual events or places or persons, living or dead, is entirely coincidental.

ALADDIN M!X

Simon & Schuster Children's Publishing Division
1230 Avenue of the Americas, New York, New York 10020
First Aladdin M!X edition March 2017
Text copyright © 2017 by Allison Gutknecht
Cover illustration copyright © 2017 by Lucy Truman
Also available in an Aladdin hardcover edition.
All rights reserved, including the right of reproduction in whole or in part in any form.
ALADDIN and related logo are registered trademarks of Simon & Schuster, Inc.
ALADDIN M!X and related logo are registered trademarks of Simon & Schuster, Inc.
For information about special discounts for bulk purchases, please contact Simon & Schuster Special Sales at 1-866-506-1949 or business@simonandschuster.com.
The Simon & Schuster Speakers Bureau can bring authors to your live event.
For more information or to book an event contact the Simon & Schuster Speakers Bureau at 1-866-248-3049 or visit our website at www.simonspeakers.com.
Cover designed by Jessica Handelman
Interior designed by Mike Rosamilia
The text of this book was set in Arno Pro.
Manufactured in the United States of America 0217 OFF
2 4 6 8 10 9 7 5 3 1
Library of Congress Control Number 2016960640
ISBN 978-1-4814-7154-1 (hc)
ISBN 978-1-4814-7153-4 (pbk)
ISBN 978-1-4814-7155-8 (eBook)

For
Nicole Oddo Smith
and
Annie Haskell McGuire,
the original residents of
the infamous Room 609

SPRING Break MISTAKE

CHAPTER 1

The worst thing about my sister is her smile.

It's not that it's a bad smile—it's a great smile, actually. One of the best there is. It's the kind of smile that seems ever-present, even when Arden is scowling. I would think the expression "she can light up a room" was a load of baloney, if it weren't for Arden's sparkle of a mouth. And the worst part is she didn't even do anything to deserve it—not really, anyway. She was gifted with picket fence–straight teeth, with a coat of white shine to match.

I, however, have the kind of teeth that require four years of braces just for the mere hope that they might someday end up not being an abject disaster. This is the injustice of my life.

Arden is flashing one of her signature smiles toward me at the moment, all while lounging on my window seat with her feet propped up on the grids of the glass pane.

Which she knows I hate.

"Get your hooves off my window," I tell her, scrolling absentmindedly through the PhotoReady app on my phone. "You're smudging my view."

"I'd hardly call this a view," Arden argues. "A bunch of trees and a rusty old swing set." I click out of PhotoReady and open the camera, aiming it in Arden's direction.

"Say cheese," I coo in a singsong voice. I pretend to snap a picture as Arden turns her head in my direction. Her feet fly off the window as she scrambles to stand.

"Don't you dare post that." She leaps across the room and flops onto the bed next to me. I roll in the opposite direction until my feet hit the floor, phone still in my hand, then I walk to the window and make a great display of lifting one of the throw pillows to clean her toe print off the glass. But at the last second, I snap a photo of it instead.

"Um, what are you doing?" Arden asks.

"Taking a picture of the mark your man-toes made,"

I say. "It could probably be studied in the Museum of Natural History."

Arden crosses her arms and stomps her foot against my bedspread. "Delete the photo," she tells me in her best principal voice. "Now."

"Oh, calm down," I tell her, settling onto the window seat and texting the toe-print shot to my best friend, Celia, with the caption, *For your heart collection*, before quickly deleting it.

"Prove you erased it," Arden says, reaching for my phone. I toss it on the bed beside her and watch her examine my albums. Satisfied, she slides it away from her. "Here's a rule for Florida—only take good pictures of me." I snort. "Or better yet, don't take pictures of me at all. That's the only way I'll know I'm safe. I mean, the worst pictures of me ever taken are the ones from spring break." Arden pulls at the ends of her thick, dark curls, twirling one around her finger. It is true that every single year, the second Arden steps off the plane and into the Florida humidity, her hair frizzes up like a beehive. What is *not* true is that this frizz results in bad pictures of her— maybe slightly worse than usual, but still not bad.

After all, she has that smile.

In contrast to Arden's mane, my hair only seems to grow limper in the Florida heat. Really, between our teeth and our hair, no one would ever believe Arden and I were sisters. As wild and unruly as Arden's hair is, mine is equally as fine and straight. "Strawberry blond" is what everyone calls it, though in the wrong light, it tends to look baby pink, like the color of a newborn girl's nursery.

And for some reason, the Florida sun is definitely the "wrong light" for my hair.

"Well, I'm sure the Backgammon Bandits and the Pinochle Posse won't mind me taking *their* pictures," I say.

Arden sighs. "What's the point of living in Florida if you don't live on the beach?" she asks. "Or at least *near* a beach."

"Or near Disney World," I add. "I'd settle for Disney World." Our grandparents have managed to pick the only place in Florida that is far from a beach, far from Disney World, and far from anything but their own retirement community. When Arden and I were little, the place seemed like a giant adventure. Our grandparents' home became our private village for the week, complete with pools and tennis courts and mysterious games like croquet and shuffleboard. But after twelve years of this annual spring break trip, I had had about all I could handle of backgammon and pinochle.

I walk across the room to retrieve my phone, and then I open PhotoReady again. At the very top of my feed is Arden's toe print—Celia has posted it with the label #CeliaHeartsNYC, courtesy of @AvalonByTheC. I smirk, more grateful than ever that Arden doesn't have a PhotoReady account. I'm sure she wouldn't be pleased to know that her enormous feet marks got a featured mention in Celia's photography project.

"What're you smiling at?" Arden asks.

"Celia's comment on my picture of Jelly," I lie.

Arden rolls her eyes. "You two and your dumb cat photos . . . ," she says, sliding herself off my bed. "I'll leave you alone to be weird by yourself." I climb onto my mattress the second Arden is gone, lying on my back with my knees bent. I hold my phone over my face, flipping through people's pictures. Without Arden, my room is so quiet that when my phone dings with a new e-mail, I nearly drop it on my nose.

I sit up to open my inbox, and three words catch my eye instantly: *Congratulations from PhotoReady!* Suddenly anxious, my fingers seem to move in slow motion as I open the body of the e-mail:

Dear Avalon Kelly,

Congratulations! You have been selected to take part in this year's junior high PhotoReady retreat (the "PhotoRetreat") in New York City!

My eyes only land on every third word as I read, the entire e-mail beginning to swim together into a gigantic blur. I start pacing the floor in a semicircle, around my bed, from one wall to the other, and then back. I hold my phone in front of me, hoping that with every lap, I'll be better able to concentrate on its contents, but I only seem to grow more nervous.

Celia and I had applied to this PhotoRetreat—a one-week getaway to New York for seventh- and eighth-grade PhotoReady users—a few months ago. For consideration, you had to use the app to create your own photo project, which is how #CeliaHeartsNYC came to be. Celia had made it her mission to photograph hearts she found "in the wild"—those created by the cream in our science teacher's coffee, or by two perfectly folded book pages, or in the snow or with sidewalk chalk, or from a bent toilet paper roll. Celia was determined for

6

us to both get accepted into the PhotoRetreat, because "how much fun would it be to spend a week in New York City *together*?" And while the retreat sounded exciting in theory, in practice, the whole thing made me uneasy. A week away from home, in a new city, with new people, and completely foreign routines? As much as I loved PhotoReady, did I really love it enough to justify five full days away from my comfort zone?

When Celia and I were both wait-listed a few weeks ago, part of me had been relieved. After all, Celia couldn't say I hadn't tried—I had created my own photo project just like she had. Mine was called #IfYouJustSmile, and I had taken close-ups of different parts of my face and then posted two pictures side by side: one where I hadn't been smiling, and another where I had. It showed the squint of my eyes, the crinkles along the sides of my nose, the indentations around my mouth, all of which formed the second I smiled. But in the pictures, I had never actually shown my mouth. Because we already know the problem there.

I sit down on the window seat, tapping my fingernails against the back of my phone. Arden is right—this view isn't exciting. It's sweet, but it's not exciting. The views in

New York City would be exciting. The pictures I could take in New York? They would be amazing. It would be a huge opportunity. It would be something I'd be stupid to turn down, to ignore, to delete the e-mail.

It could be fun.

It could be fun, at least, if Celia were there too.

I moan out loud to myself, taking my phone out from under my legs and opening the camera. Aiming the lens out the window, to the same backyard I've seen nearly every day of my life, I center the abandoned swing set and snap a picture. I then open PhotoReady, load the shot into a frame, choose the black-and-white filter, and type a caption: *Old view*.

And as I watch the photo load onto my screen, I wonder if I'm ready to start looking at something new.

CHAPTER 2

I march across the hall to Arden's room and head directly to her wicker rocking chair. Collapsing into it, I announce, "I need to tell you something."

Arden rotates around to face me, a questioning look in her arched eyebrows.

"Wait a second," I begin, dropping my phone on the rocking chair to go shut her door.

"This sounds serious," Arden says.

"It is."

"Did Jelly side-swipe a vase again? Mom can't keep claiming that every vase is her favorite. This is getting ridic—"

"Not about Jelly. About me," I say, returning to the rocker.

"Go on," Arden says, crossing her arms against her chest and leaning back in her seat. Arden is a year younger than me, but we've always acted more like twins—twins who look nothing alike, but twins nonetheless. As if I'm only three minutes older than her, instead of thirteen months. She is mostly my best friend, even more than Celia is—which means she can also drive me battier than anyone else in the world.

But for times like these, she's exactly who I need.

"So . . . ," I begin. "I told you how Celia and I applied for that PhotoReady retreat a few months ago? The one they're doing in New York the week of our spring break?"

"Weren't you wait-listed? Which you decided was their nice way of rejecting you?"

"Yes," I say. "Only we were *actually* wait-listed. And now, I'm . . . not wait-listed."

Arden's eyes widen. "You got in?"

I nod my head slowly. "They just sent me an e-mail."

"No way!" Arden shouts, leaping up from her chair.

"Shhhh." I shush her. "I don't want Mom or Dad to hear."

"Why? That's awesome! I guess you're more talented with that silly camera than I give you credit for." She says this last part with a smirk.

"I'm not sure I'm going to go," I confess.

"Why? A whole week in New York with your camera? Sounds right up your alley."

"Maybe if Celia were going," I say. "But I haven't heard from her, which makes me think she didn't get an e-mail. And I would never go to New York by myself."

Arden stares at me blankly, as if I'm speaking a foreign language. "Um, you have to go. This is, like, a big deal."

"No, I'm not going," I say matter-of-factly. "Unless Celia ends up going too, but otherwise, no way." The skin on my arms begins crawling with goose bumps at the thought of spending a week with a bunch of strangers, away from everything—and everyone—I know.

"Seriously? We were just complaining about having to spend another spring break at the Retirement Ranch. This is your chance to finally do something different."

"You'd want to suffer alone with the Pinochle Posse?" I ask.

"Of course not," Arden answers. "But that doesn't mean you shouldn't go to New York."

It's my turn to be surprised. "That's awfully generous of you," I tell her.

"Oh yes, that's my middle name: Generosity," Arden retorts. "Arden Generosity Kelly."

"Okay, you're no help to me." I stand up to leave, but Arden blocks my path.

"You have to do it," she says in her most serious voice. "You love taking pictures. You love New York."

"We've only been there twice," I point out.

"Yes, and both were over the holiday break," Arden says. "You know what they say—if you can love New York during tourist season, you can love it anytime."

"Who says that?"

"Everyone. Now promise me you'll go. Whether Celia does or not. You will go."

"I can't promise that," I say. "What am I supposed to do—sneak off to New York and hope Celia shows up too? I can't go without her, but I also can't ask her if she got in."

"But you can tell her that *you* did," Arden says. "Let me see that e-mail." I hand her my phone with the letter displayed across the screen.

"'Dear Avalon Kelly,'" Arden reads out loud. "Sounds so official."

"Please don't read it to me," I beg, and Arden scans the rest in silence before fiddling with my phone. When she gives it back to me, Celia's face is on the screen—the picture that pops up whenever I call her, or she calls me.

"Here," Arden says. "Talk to her. She's your best friend. She should be happy for you." Before I can protest, I hear a faint "Hello?" coming from the phone. Celia's voice. I mouth a silent *I hate you* to Arden before darting out of her room and back to my own.

"Hello?" Celia repeats.

"Hey, sorry," I say, shutting the door behind me. "I was running out of Arden's room."

"No problem," Celia says. "What's up?"

I think about how to answer. I suppose Arden is right—I can't keep this news from Celia forever. Especially not now that I've told Arden, who is *never* going to let me keep it a secret.

"So I got an e-mail," I begin.

"Mmm-hmm," Celia says, sounding distracted.

"From PhotoReady," I continue.

"Oh, yeah?" Celia asks, a little more interested.

"About the retreat. Did . . . did you get one?"

"No," Celia answers. "What about the retreat?"

I sit on my bed stiffly, as if bracing for impact. "I got in."

There are a few seconds of silence on the other end of the phone, and then a few more. The quiet goes on for so long that I'm convinced the connection must have failed.

"Celia?" I finally ask.

"I'm here," she says. "Wow. That's . . . great."

"But listen . . ." I begin talking quickly. "You should totally be the one to go—*you're* the one who found out about the retreat. I'll tell them I want to transfer my invitation to you."

"No." Celia stops me. "You can't do that. It said all over the application that invitations were nontransferable."

"Oh," I say. "Then I'll decline it, and maybe they'll let you in instead. Maybe they only want one person per town, so if I say I'm not going—"

"You don't have to do that," Celia interrupts me. "You should go if you want to."

"But I don't, not without you," I tell her. "Promise."

"You shouldn't give up your spot. That would be a waste."

"Well, maybe you'll still get in." I try to say this hopefully.

"Maybe," Celia says, sounding about as confident as I do.

"And if you do, we can still go together," I say. "You know, if our parents agree and everything. But if you don't, I won't go either. I don't even want to go—it wouldn't be fun without you."

"'Kay," Celia says absentmindedly. "Listen, I've got to have dinner. I'll talk to—"

"I'm not going on the retreat," I insist before she can hang up. "I'm going to write back and say *no, thank you.* Plus, it's next week—it's not like they gave me much warning. I already have plans."

"Don't do that. Not yet," Celia says. "Going to your grandparents' lame retirement home doesn't count as 'plans.' No offense. And like you said, maybe I'll still get in. And then we really can go together. Give it a few more days."

"But I don't even want to go," I say.

"You're *scared* to go," Celia tells me. "But I think you *want* to. That's different. Hey, now I really do have to hang up. Just please don't say no yet. Let's see what happens." The line goes silent.

I toss my phone onto the pillow next to me and trace

the pattern on my bedspread with the tip of my finger. I had thought keeping the news to myself would be harder than sharing it, but now, the more people that find out, the more nervous I feel.

And the more I wish I had never applied to the PhotoRetreat in the first place.

CHAPTER 3

By the next morning, I have completely talked myself out of even considering going to New York. A whole night of being woken up by my own carousel of thoughts—spinning round and round without an off switch—convinced me that if I'm *this* anxious about the retreat now, then the only solution is to avoid it entirely.

I open PhotoReady out of habit while walking toward the stairs. A flurry of notifications greets me in the corner of the screen, along with a bright red private message icon. Every single notification is from the username @SofiaNoPH—and she seems to have starred at least half of my pictures overnight. I stand at the top of the steps to open the message, confused.

Hi there!

This is superawkward, but it looks
like I'm your roommate for the
PhotoRetreat in New York! I'm soooooo
excited to get there, and to meet you!
Your pictures are beyond star-worthy—
you have a really great eye (sorry if
that sounds like I think I'm a big shot.
I promise I don't usually talk like that.
What I mean is YOUR PICTURES ARE
AWESOME).

Anyway, hope you write me back so I
don't feel like a big loser.

PS: How do you say your name? Like
AYVA with a LON on the end? I don't
want to call you the wrong thing when I
meet you—talk about superawkward.

xoxo, Sofia (@SofiaNoPH) from Arizona

I hightail it back to my room and begin pacing, the same jitters from yesterday having returned even more intensely.

"Arden!" I yell. Arden appears in my doorway seconds later.

"What's with the shouting?"

"Look," I say in a hushed voice, holding out my phone for her to see. "The retreat already paired me with a roommate. And the roommate sent me a note. What do I do now?"

"Wow, she's from Arizona?" Arden asks. "Think about how far away New York must seem to her. And you're being a big baby about going a few minutes up the turnpike."

"A few minutes? It's like two hours."

"But this girl—what's her name? Sofia?—she has to fly on a plane for, like, what, two days? If she can do it, you can do it."

"Um, it doesn't take two days to fly to Arizona," I correct her.

"I was exaggerating for effect."

"Why are you being so pushy about this?" I ask. "I thought you'd be on my side."

"I *am* on your side. That's the whole point. I know what's better for you more than you do," Arden says. "Even if it's worse for me."

"You're not helping," I tell her. "Just, never mind. Forget I ever said anything."

"You have to answer her," Arden tells me. "You can't be rude."

"And say what? That I'm not actually coming on the retreat?"

"I thought you and Celia decided you'd give it a few days," Arden says.

"But isn't that worse? To pretend I'm coming and then back out? That seems mean."

"Meaner than not responding at all? I don't think so," Arden says, turning to leave. "Answer the poor girl. I could use a friend in Arizona."

"You?"

"Sure," Arden says. "I'd like a friend in every state. It will make my college road trip much easier."

"You're in sixth grade," I remind her.

"Never too early to start planning," Arden calls as she strolls toward her room. I roll my eyes and bury my face against my pillow. Arden is right—I can't be rude. So before I can talk myself out of it, I open Sofia's message again and rapidly type a response:

Hi Sofia,

Wow, your pictures are amazing too! Arizona looks so much more interesting than New Jersey!

To be honest, I'm not sure if I'm attending the retreat yet. I just got off the wait list yesterday, so it's kind of a new thing. But no matter what, thanks for contacting me. I followed you so I can see all the pictures you post from New York City!

<3, Avalon (@AvalonByTheC)

PS: Oh, and my name is pronounced exactly like it looks, but with a short *A* sound at the beginning. I was named after a beach town in New Jersey (which is where my PhotoReady name came from, too).

I press send before I can agonize over the response—
or my decision about the retreat—any longer.

Celia is standing at my locker when I reach the seventh-
grade hallway, hunched over her phone in concentration.

"Hey," I greet her.

"Who's this girl who's starring all your PhotoReady
pictures?" she asks immediately.

"How did you see that already?"

"She also commented on like every single one. It
wasn't hard to notice," Celia says.

I twist out my locker combination, not making eye
contact. "She was assigned as my roommate. For the
retreat." I pull books out of my bag and deposit them on
my locker shelf.

"You already have a roommate? Wow, they don't
waste much time."

"I mean, it's in less than a week. They sent out the
e-mail about roommates late last night. Sofia must have
looked up my account," I explain.

"Sofia is the name of the stalker?"

"She's not a stalker," I say. "She seems nice." I pull out
the books I need for first and second periods and begin

walking toward our homeroom, Celia following behind me with her nose stuck to her phone screen.

"If you trip and fall walking like that, I'm not going to help you," I warn her. "Anyway, I already told her that I wasn't going on the retreat. So you can stop being a Sofia hater."

"Did she respond?"

"Yes. She wrote 'No' with about ninety-seven Os," I say. "I haven't replied to that yet."

Celia and I turn into our homeroom. "You should go," she tells me. "Really. Then I can live the retreat in your body, or whatever that's called."

"Vicariously," I fill in. "But no, I'm not going without you."

"But you'll have Sofia," Celia says in a singsong voice. "Your new best friend."

"Quit it," I say. "Seriously, I'm not going. My parents probably wouldn't let me go anyway. PhotoReady didn't exactly give me much notice."

"Hold on, you didn't tell your parents yet?"

"No. I'll tell them tonight. And they'll say 'no' and that will be the end of it."

Celia steps in front of me to face me head-on. "Listen,

if you go, at least I'll feel like I'm there too. You'll send me constant updates. You won't even have to talk to anyone else, you'll be so busy texting me."

The bell rings, and Celia and I shuffle to our seats. I pull out my phone and open PhotoReady, Sofia's *Nooooooooooooooooo!* flashing across the screen. I type back a fast reply.

> What were you doing up so early anyway?
> Wasn't it like five a.m. in Arizona?

I close our messages and return to Sofia's profile, opening one of her selfies. She has midnight-dark hair, with thick bangs parading across her forehead, and her skin looks permanently tanned, which I suppose makes sense for someone who lives in the Arizona sunshine. Before I can look at another shot, a red message balloon pops up on my screen.

> I have a seminocturnal dog. At least, she's nocturnal whenever she wants me to get up and give her a drink in the middle of the night.

What's this about you not coming on the
retreat??? You HAVE to come! You're
clearly not a weirdo—and what if you
don't come and then they stick me with
a weirdo????? Really, you'd be doing me
a favor—plus, we'd have the BEST time!
I've never been to New York—have you?

I throw my phone in my bag without answering,
organizing my notebooks as the first-period bell rings.

"Who have you been texting? Your stalker?" Celia
appears at my desk out of nowhere, and I jump slightly
at the sight of her.

"Very funny," I say, following her out into the hallway.
We make our way to Science, Celia scrolling through her
phone the whole time.

"Oh, for the love . . ." She raises her voice over the din
of the hallway. "Now you tell me this girl isn't obsessed
with you." Celia shoves her phone in front of my face, so
close to my eyes that the image is blurry. I take it from
her and Sofia comes into focus. She's sitting on top of a
huge purple plastic suitcase and holding a piece of paper
with *Less Than One Week Until the PhotoRetreat!!!* written

25

in bubble letters. Underneath the picture, Sofia has captioned it: *Can't wait to get to NYC and meet my absolutely nonweirdo roommate, @AvalonByTheC! See, Avalon, now it's official—you can't back out now!*

Oh, brother.

CHAPTER 4

I thought my parents would shoot down the idea of the PhotoRetreat immediately.

I thought they would say it was too soon, too expensive, too dangerous.

I thought I would be able to blame them for passing up the opportunity, for disappointing Sofia, for having yet another boring spring break.

I thought wrong.

Not only did my parents not say no to the Photo-Retreat, they all but insisted I go.

"We will all be nervous, I'm sure," Mom had said. "But we would be silly to let you walk away from this, Avalon. It's a huge honor that you got in."

"I only got in off the wait list," I had pointed out. "Probably after someone else backed out."

"That doesn't matter. What matters is that you're in now. And you're going." The decision made for me, I could now be found in our living room the night before I was scheduled to leave, surrounded by dozens of bags from Mom's and my shopping excursion at Knickknacks and Whatnots. PhotoReady is putting all the retreat participants up in college dorm rooms for the five days and four nights we're there, with all the essentials already provided (a bed, mattress, desk, lamp, trash can, dresser, plus a bathroom *inside* the room, which Mom said was a real dorm luxury). All we had to bring were sheets, towels, toiletries, clothes (of course), and anything else we needed to make our rooms feel "homey."

Which to Mom meant half the inventory of Knickknacks and Whatnots.

The doorbell rings, and I scale over the bags to reach our front door. When I open it, I find Celia standing on our porch, the smallest gift bag of all time in her hand.

"Where did you find that, gift wrapping for elves?" I ask when she gives it to me.

"Wouldn't elves be quite good at gift wrapping?" Celia asks. "What with Santa's workshop and all?"

"Fine, gift wrapping for gnomes," I correct myself. "Are gnomes small?"

"Let's say they are," Celia agrees. When I hear it out loud, our conversation sounds completely normal—exactly how we always talk. But underneath the surface, there is something else. Something a little bit uncomfortable, or forced. I've noticed this ever since the day I told Celia I had, in fact, decided—or really, my parents had decided for me—to go to New York after all. She said she was happy for me. She said how exciting it was. She said she couldn't wait to hear all about it.

But the pinch in the corners of her eyes said something different.

I tear into the gift bag, and my hand emerges clutching a small key chain. The letter *A* is on one side, and *C* is on the other, with beach waves crashing in the background.

"It's from Atlantic City," Celia explains. "But I thought it was a good token to represent your PhotoReady trip. Get it—'Avalon by the C,' like your username," she says.

"It's awesome," I tell her sincerely. "I'm going to use it for my dorm key. Thank you."

"Sure," Celia says. "Just swear that you won't dump me for that stalker Sofia."

"She's not a stalk . . ." I begin to defend her, but Celia's face tells me that's not what she needs to hear right now. "I won't," I say instead.

"You better not," Celia says. "It's not like having a best friend all the way in Arizona would be useful anyway." She walks to the door. "So you promise?"

"Promise what?"

"Not to replace me," Celia says. "Or forget about me once you meet all your brand-new NYC besties."

"I guarantee that won't happen," I say. "I'll be texting you the whole time. You know how much I enjoy talking to new people . . . ." I roll my eyes.

"Good. Keep it that way." Celia nods with satisfaction. "I mean, have fun or whatever, but not too much. And keep me posted. Like hourly. Minute by minute would be better."

"I will," I say. "Literally. I'll keep you 'posted.' Get it? Like PhotoReady posts?"

"Save your puns for Sofia," Celia tells me. I stand on our porch as she walks away.

"Hey, look," I call after her, pointing to the sky. One

of the last clouds of the day is shaped like something that, if stared at from the right angle, could totally look like a heart. Celia glances up and gives a small smile.

"Cute," she calls, continuing down the sidewalk.

But I can't help but notice that she doesn't snap a photo of it, just like she hasn't posted a single #CeliaHeartsNYC picture in days.

I twirl my key chain around my finger, worrying. At first, I thought it was only the week ahead of me about which I had to be concerned. I never thought that what I had to return home to might be equally uncertain.

The following morning, I sit in the backseat with Arden as Dad drives us up the New Jersey Turnpike to Manhattan. The two times we had come to the city when I was younger, we had ridden the train, and Dad's current tense driving feels as skittish as my jumpy insides. I wonder if it's too late to make my family take me to Florida with them instead, to turn this whole trip around and head south. As I watch the view out the window shift from the generic greens of the trees along the guardrails, to the low-flying planes descending upon Newark Airport, to the smoky oil refineries of North Jersey, the phantom wiggling worms inside me seem to grow more restless, until any plan other than showing up at the retreat seems like a better one.

"Ugh, this is why everyone thinks New Jersey is ugly," Arden pipes up next to me. She gestures toward the window, to the power lines and smog that overwhelm the scenery. "You would think they could've run the turnpike through a more appealing part of the state."

"Let them think that—more room for us," Dad says. But as they speak, my family's conversation seems to morph into an indecipherable chorus, as if I've dived into a pool and the world around me is still there, but suddenly gone, all at the same time.

Because right there, out my window, peeking through the billows of smoke, is New York City. From this distance, it looks almost fake—like something built from LEGOs. Through the foggy air, the skyline rises as if it were within a frame at the art museum, right there but also somehow imaginary. I don't remember noticing any of this during my previous arrivals—I guess the view from the train never caught my attention in the same way. But as I raise my phone to try to capture the sight with my camera, something—either the bumps in the road or the shake of my own fingers—causes the image to blur. I pull up the "best" of the pictures and type a quick text to Sofia: *Look what I found (please don't hold the photo quality against me).*

Arghhh!!!!! Sofia writes back almost immediately. *I was JUST going to text you—I landed a few minutes ago! I am sooooooo excited to get to our room . . . and to finally meet YOU!*

Me too, I write with a smiley face. *Well, I'm excited to meet you. But I'm also really, really nervous. Like, ridiculously.*

Don't be nervous. I promise I'm fun.

Hahaha, I have no doubt. But I still feel jittery.

Keep sending me pictures, Sofia says. *Give me the full tour since I'm sure you'll get there before me. Remember, this is the first time I'm seeing New York!*

I'll try, I tell her. *But I'm too shaky to capture anything PhotoReady-worthy right now!*

Look at the quote in my profile, Sofia writes back. *That's my motto for the week.* I open PhotoReady, tapping on @SofiaNoPH's profile. There, under her name, is a new quote—one I've never seen before: *I photograph what scares me. I photograph the things I scare.*

Who said that? I type to Sofia.

Me. Does it sound too pretentious?

No, it's brilliant, I assure her. *Give me a second, and*

then look at my profile. I swipe back to my own Photo-Ready account and click to edit my profile. Under my name, I place in quotation marks, *I photograph what scares me. I photograph the things I scare.* And then I add —*@SofiaNoPH*. I save it and then wait for Sofia's reaction.

Hahahahaha, I receive a minute later. *You are too kind.* I look up and realize we're on the loop approaching the Lincoln Tunnel, only the Hudson River separating me from New York.

I can see the tunnel. . . . I tell her.

SO CLOSE! Just think—you're only a few blocks away from the best week of our lives!

"Are you excited, Avalon?" Mom calls from the front.

"I'm not sure," I say quietly, which immediately causes Arden to smack my arm.

"Get excited!" she yells. "I'm excited, and I'm the one who has to spend the whole week with the Pinochle Posse." As Dad pulls our car through the tollbooth and into the entrance of the tunnel, my phone vibrates again. I look down, expecting a new text from Sofia. But instead, I find Celia's name staring up at me, with only two words underneath: *Nice quote.*

CHAPTER 5

I'm so distracted by Celia's text that I nearly miss our entrance to the city. Arden hits me on the arm again as Dad pulls our car through the arched opening at the other end of the tunnel, my eyes squinting as they adjust from the dim light to the brightness of . . . New York.

"Do me a favor—look up every once in a while," Arden says. "You would have missed the big reveal if it weren't for me!"

"Yeah, thanks," I say, shielding my eyes to look at my surroundings. In all honesty, the area outside the tunnel is less magical-looking than I would have hoped. The car lanes immediately become rough guidelines, as Dad dodges three taxis and an overaggressive minivan in his attempts to merge over to the downtown exit. He jerks us down the street, muttering to himself before smacking his palm against the center of the horn, a loud blare ringing out through the city.

"Dad, really?" Arden calls.

"These people don't know how to drive," Dad says.

"And you're becoming one of them," Mom tells him.

Might never make it to the dorm, I type to Sofia. *My dad is trying to get us all killed.*

Yes, well, my taxi driver doesn't seem to be doing much better! Sofia answers. *Also, HOLY TRAFFIC. I can still see the airport over my shoulder. ARGHHH!*

"We're almost there, I think," Dad tells us, the car's navigation system directing us through the city streets.

"Sofia requests that she have a roommate with a pulse," I say. "So no more Mr. Toad's Wild Ride driving necessary."

"New York is already making you snarky, I see," Dad calls back. "And, hey, look who got us here in one piece, despite you three backseat drivers!" He slides our car into a space beside the curb, and I look up to find the sign for Morningview Dormitory outside the window.

And I freeze.

It's not that the dorm doesn't look welcoming—okay, actually, it doesn't. It looks like the outside of a nursing home, but one that was built before the term "nursing home" existed. Its brick façade, which might have been red in the 1800s, has turned a dusty shade of gray, the bricks in need of a good power-washing. And the entrance, well, that's another issue. The canopy leading to the front door isn't exactly ripped, but it may or may not have been "stitched" back together with duct tape. And while what's through the front door isn't visible from my window, I *can* tell that it looks like one thing: dark. The kind of dismal dreariness that arrives right before a summer rainstorm, covering the world in a blanket of dingy mist.

That's what this dorm should be called: Dingymist Dormitory. "Morningview" it is not.

"Here we go!" Dad sounds ten times more enthusiastic than I feel as he swings open the driver's-side door. "If this doesn't look like a real New York City college experience, I don't know what does!"

"Remind me to pick a school in the suburbs," I murmur under my breath, opening my own door reluctantly. Mom, Dad, and Arden are already gathered at the trunk, pulling out the plethora of bags from Knickknacks and Whatnots. As they pile my belongings along the curb, a deafening sound appears behind me, growing louder and louder, like the dangerous rumblings of your neighbor's illegal fireworks. I dive off the sidewalk without turning around, trying to hover for safety behind Dad, all without *looking* like I'm hovering for safety behind Dad.

"Hi there!" a voice calls as the thunderous sound comes to a sudden halt. "Moving in for the Photo-Retreat?" I peer from behind Dad's back to find a perfectly innocent-looking pair of teenagers—college students?—standing over a giant blue bin on wheels.

"*She* is," Arden answers, pointing in my direction. "Avalon Kelly."

The girl in the duo scrolls through the papers attached to the clipboard in her hand. "Yes, here you are, great!" she says. "You're in room six-oh-nine. The counselor in charge of your area should be up there to assist in getting you settled—her name is Ella. Family, feel free to help Avalon to her room, but then we're encouraging parents and siblings to make a fast exit, and let our retreaters unpack with their roommates. You know, for bonding and all that."

Mom and Dad both nod as if this makes perfect sense, and Arden begins plopping bag after bag into the blue cart. The boy of the duo hands Dad a sign for the windshield of his car—eligible for thirty minutes of parking only, which really does mean they'll have to leave quickly.

And then, I'll be alone.

I fiddle with my phone as Mom fills out some paperwork—signing my life away to the ghosts of Dingymist Dorm, most likely.

"Why am I the only one doing the heavy lifting around here?" Arden interrupts my thoughts. "Move it or lose it." I take the last bag from the trunk and place it on top of the overflowing bin.

"There, I helped," I tell her.

"Did you bring your phone charger?" she asks.

"Nice time to remind me," I say. "If I claim I didn't, do you think I can leave?"

"Right, because I'm sure all your fellow PhotoReady addicts wouldn't have one to spare," Arden says. She begins rolling the cart toward the ramp leading to the front door, putting every ounce of her weight behind it. "Seriously, you're just going to stand there?" she calls over her shoulder. I help her maneuver the cart up the ramp and through the front door, only to find a lobby that somehow looks even worse up close. We steer the bin past the unsmiling security guard and onto the waiting elevator.

"We only have thirty minutes to unload you, Avalon," Dad says as we rise.

"I heard," I tell him curtly. "Let's get this over with." When we reach the sixth floor, I exit the elevator and find another counselor waiting in the vestibule.

"Hello!" She is just as chipper, if not more so, as the two downstairs. "Do you know what room you're headed to?"

"Uh, six-oh-nine," I answer.

"Oh, perfecto!" she says, extending her hand toward mine to shake. "I'm Ella, your dormitory chaperone for the week."

"I'm Avalon," I reply shyly.

"Oh, you're Avalon," Ella says. "I was wondering whose face would be attached to that name. It's so pretty."

"Thank you," I say. "Or, I guess, thank my parents." I point to my family, who has rolled up behind me with the cart. "Since I didn't pick it."

Ella laughs at this, but there is something so robustly perky about her that I can't tell whether she means it or not. "Let me show you to your room," she says. "I think you're the first to arrive."

"Yes, Sofia is on her way from the airport," I say.

"So you guys have already been in contact?" Ella asks, and I nod. "Perfecto!"

I haven't even known this girl a full minute yet, and she's already said "perfecto" twice. "Perkyfecto" was more like it.

We make our way down the hall until we reach the door with the numbers 609 hanging across its center. "Here we are!" Ella calls, riffling through her key ring until she finds one labeled with the same number. She removes it and hands it to me. "Would you like to do the honors?"

"Um, sure," I say, and I unlock the door to find a bare room, with little more than a bunk bed, two mattresses, two desks, and a couple of chairs. I immediately wish I weren't the first to arrive, that Sofia could have gotten here first and made this place look more like a home and less like a prison cell.

I also wish that my family would leave immediately,

without even kissing me good-bye. That they would head downstairs and take Ella with them, leaving me with this huge bin of stuff and this tiny room, in order to deal, all on my own, with the tears that are stinging the backs of my eyes.

CHAPTER 6

I avoid eye contact with everyone as we unload the contents of the cart, in case the film of tears is visible. Thankfully, it doesn't take long before the bin is empty, and I have been boxed into the room by Knickknacks and Whatnots bags.

Which also means that I'm about to be left by myself in this strange place with these strange people, none of whom—not even Sofia—I really know. Not like how I know my family, or Celia, or anyone whose presence is as comforting to me as a preschooler's teddy bear. Ella flits out of the room so that we "can say a proper good-bye" (a "perfecto" good-bye, I'm sure is what she means), and my parents both give me a tight, suffocating hug.

"Remember to keep us updated," Mom says. "I'll contact Sofia if you're not responding to my proof-of-life requests. Or Ella—I now have her number too."

"Be careful, but have the best time," Dad says, backing out of the room and pulling Mom along with him. "Arden, we'll be in the hall. Make it quick."

And as much as I managed to hold it together in front of my parents, the minute the door closes and I'm left with only my sister, my eyes sprinkle with tears, my cheeks scrunching sideways into the telltale sign that a sob is about to escape.

"Hey, HEY." Arden grabs me by my shoulders and gives me a small shake. "Snap out of it. You're in New York. People come from all over the world to see this place once, for one day, and you get to be here—to *live* here—a full week."

"I know," I manage to mutter through a gasp of tears. "But—"

"Nope." Arden cuts me off. "I'm the one who should be crying. I'm the one about to head off to *Golden Girls* Land. You? You're the lucky one." She raps two soft pats against my cheek. "Plus, you know you're the *big* sister, right? You're supposed to be the role model here. Buck up, chump."

Despite myself, I laugh at the serious expression on Arden's face, which makes her break into one of her famous grins. "That's more like it," she says. "I'm not going to hug you because I'd rather not have a shoulder full of snot for our entire flight. So, you know, text me and everything. And for the record, I'm still not joining PhotoReady, so don't expect me to look at your pictures all week. Just send me the ones that you think I won't hate." I nod as Arden marches toward the door, calling a casual "Ta-ta" as it closes behind her.

And then . . . silence.

I wipe the backs of my hands across my eyelids, trying to pull myself together. With the tissue box that we purchased buried in the Knickknacks and Whatnots rubble, I begin to dig through the bags in desperation. Luckily, I find the box in the third bag, and I pull out three tissues at once. I blow my nose harshly, and then I begin dumping the rest of the bags' contents onto the bottom mattress. But looking at all the stuff at once makes me feel overwhelmed, so instead, I find the bag with my phone and tap out a text to Sofia.

I'm here. Do you have a preference on the top or bottom

bunk? I sit on the surface of one of the desks—one of the only clear areas left in the room—to wait for her response.

If you don't mind, bottom would be better for me, Sofia writes back. *I have kind of a heights thing. How's the room???*

I swoop my eyes from one end of the space to the other, trying to think of how to describe it. Every angle I turn, the bare walls stare back at me, quiet in their blankness.

It's, I begin to type, but then Sofia's words pop into my head: *I photograph what scares me. I photograph the things I scare.* I open my camera and begin taking pictures of the room, rather than describing it with words. I photograph the bunk bed—the twists and turns of the metal coils, and the sea foam–green mattresses. Then I head to the bathroom, standing in the middle of our tub to try to capture the whole room at once. Afterward, I stand in the bedroom's threshold, aiming my camera toward the front door. I snap a picture of the vague glimmer of the doorknob against the darkness of the door itself, and then I reposition my camera to try to capture the upper corners of the frame.

And without warning, the door flies open, startling

me to the point that a scream—an honest-to-goodness scream—escapes from my mouth.

"SURPRISE!" the person in the doorway bellows. And even if her PhotoReady account hadn't shown me what she looks like, I'd somehow know Sofia anywhere. She pushes the door open wider so that it bangs against the wall, and she flings herself into the room.

"You scared me *to death*!" I yell, but despite the fact that my heart is beating so hard that I can feel it in the back of my head, I find myself laughing. Sofia throws her arms around my shoulders, letting the door slam behind her. I hug her back, this stranger-slash-friend. And for a moment—a small moment, but still a moment—I feel a little bit more at home.

CHAPTER 7

"Whoa," Sofia says, glancing into our bedroom. "Did you bring all of New Jersey with you?"

"Most of this would be my mom's doing," I tell her. "But speaking of bags . . ."

"Oh, right," Sofia says. "I left mine in the hall. Everyone at the airport looked at me like I was nuts, but compared to your nonsense . . ." She trails off with a smile, opening our door and wheeling in not one, not two, but three suitcases. Two of them are so large that petite Sofia herself could definitely fit inside. "So, first things first—I brought my photo printer so we can begin decorating the walls with our PhotoReady shots. It's looking awfully depressing in here."

"I like your priorities," I tell her, helping to wheel one of the bags into the bedroom. And despite the small amount of time we've been in each other's company, I feel like I've known Sofia much longer. Something about her reminds me of Celia—the bubbly talkativeness, the hyper darting about. I already feel comfortable with her—much more comfortable than I ever anticipated feeling in New York.

Sofia blocks the remainder of our "hallway" by opening one of the body-size suitcases.

"So once you have that thing unpacked, we're going to see if you fit inside, right?" I ask.

"Definitely," Sofia agrees. "And then you're going to wheel me down the hall to Ella's room and tell her you can't find your roommate."

"Oh, you met her?" I ask. "How many times did she say 'perfecto'?"

Sofia's dark eyes grow wide. "Thank goodness you noticed that too. I thought someone had to have been secretly videotaping me for a prank show—it was seriously every other word out of her mouth!"

As if on cue, a knock sounds at our door, and Sofia and I fall suddenly silent.

"Do you think it's her?" she mouths to me. We tiptoe to the door and then each try to place an eye over the peephole. Since Sofia is shorter than me, we end up with our heads stacked on top of one another like a totem pole, which makes us sputter into nervous giggles, giving ourselves away to whoever is on the other side of the door.

"Avalon and Sofia?" the voice calls. "It's me, Ella. I wanted to see how you two are making out in there." Sofia unclasps the lock.

"We're starting to unpack," Sofia tells her. "We have kind of, um, a lot of stuff."

"Perfecto," Ella says, and I have to bite the insides of my cheeks to keep from laughing in her face. "Let me know if you need anything—you have until four p.m. to unpack, and then all of the retreaters are meeting in the lobby to head to an early dinner."

"Perfecto," Sofia responds, and to her great credit, not one centimeter of her face so much as crinkles. In contrast, I have to turn around to prevent the giggles from escaping, because the sight of Sofia's stone-straight face makes me want to laugh even harder. When I hear the door close, I whirl around to face her.

"I can't believe you did that," I say, letting the pent-up laughter escape in a giant fit, somehow more powerful from having had to hold it in. I sit on top of Sofia's luggage, clutching my middle. "How did you say 'perfecto' with such a straight face? And do you think she heard us talking about her when she knocked? We were right by the door."

"Nah, and even if she had, Ella doesn't strike me as the type who would have caught on," Sofia says. "I doubt she realizes that 'perfecto' is her main vocabulary word." She reaches down to her open suitcase and hauls out a box. "Have you seen an outlet anywhere?"

"Behind the desks," I point. "Good luck making your way over there." Sofia dodges our bags and places the box on an empty desktop, removing the printer.

"Do you want to plug in your phone first?" she asks.

"Sure," I say. "Should I open my photos?"

"Yep. Choose which picture you want to print, and then hit this orange button. Trust me, this is the best invention ever. It's so much faster than any other photo printer I've had."

I open my album, and the last picture I had taken

automatically fills the screen. And if I weren't seeing it with my own eyes, I swear I wouldn't believe it existed.

"Sofia," I begin, "you've got to see this." I hold my phone out to her, and her chin drops down, followed by an enormous grin.

"How did you ever capture that?" she asks. "You didn't even know I was coming—I wanted to surprise you."

"I was taking pictures of the door," I explain. "You had asked how our room was, so I wanted to show you. So when you walked in, you walked into my photo."

"Well, obviously, that's the one that needs to be printed first," Sofia says. "Since it's capturing our first meeting."

"Agreed," I say, plugging my phone into Sofia's printer and dutifully pressing the orange button. A few seconds later, the photo is in my hands, Sofia hovering next to me with a roll of double-sided tape.

"Let's put it in the middle of this blank wall, and then work out from there," Sofia suggests, pointing to the wall across from our bunks. She puts four small squares of tape into each of the corners of the printout, and then positions it in place. "I love it. How about you print out nine more photos you want to add, and then we'll switch?"

"Perfecto," I answer her, but Sofia already has her phone poised in front of our faces, ready for a selfie.

"It's our first roommate picture," she says. I place my chin near her shoulder and tilt my head toward hers, drawing my lips closed for my usual toothless smile.

"You're not going to post that, are you?" I ask once she snaps it.

"Why? We're adorable," she says, holding up the photo for me to see. And while Sofia looks just like herself—cheerful and happy to be here—my smile, or lack thereof, makes me seem like the crabby, boring roommate.

"I think we could do better," I tell her. "We'll try again later." What I really mean is next time we take a photo, I'll make sure to take it myself, and then crop out the bottom halves of our faces.

"Nah, I like this one," Sofia insists, making a great flourish as she loads it onto her feed. "Let the entire retreat see we're the best roommates." And since I suspect there's no arguing with Sofia when it comes to her PhotoReady page, I decide to let it go. "Look," she says a few seconds later, holding out her phone triumphantly.

Our photo appears with the caption *NYC BFFs!!!* I give her a thumbs-up before opening PhotoReady myself to be the first one to star it.

Slowly but surely, Sofia and I make our way through the multitude of bags littering our floor. We take turns printing pictures, while also putting sheets on our beds, placing our clothes in the dresser, bringing our toiletries to the bathroom, and displaying our snacks across the desktops (Sofia almost immediately polished off a bag of chips. For such a little thing, she sure could eat).

"Too bad we don't have beanbag chairs," Sofia says. "They'd make a great addition."

"I hate to tell you, but I'm not sure we could jam much more into this room," I say as she tries to force her three empty suitcases into the tiny closet.

"It doesn't look half-bad in here, all things considered," Sofia says. "Oh, wait! I almost forgot." She dives for her bookbag and rustles around, eventually pulling out a box of tiny lightbulbs on wired strings.

"Christmas lights?" I ask her skeptically. "It's April."

"No, twinkle lights!" Sofia says. "I mean, yes, technically, I suppose they're Christmas lights, but trust me—they're a dorm room must-have. Now where should we put them?" We both look around the room.

"How about as a 'frame' for our mural?" I suggest.

"Good idea, but that would make it harder to add more pictures to it," Sofia reasons. "Up and down our bedposts?"

"I think I'd have trouble sleeping if we kept them on at night," I say. "And I'm guessing the point is to keep them on at all times?"

"Yes, definitely," Sofia agrees. "So where? The bathroom?"

"How about around the windows?" I suggest.

"Yes!" Sofia exclaims. "Let's do it." We each climb onto a desk and begin draping the lights across the top of the windows, securing them with Sofia's tape. We cascade them down the two sides of the panes, bringing the ends together along the bottom—a perfect fit.

"I love this so much," Sofia says. "I'm going to take a picture of it to add to our mural. This has to be the best-looking room in all of Morningview Dormitory."

"Oh, I meant to tell you—I think it should be called Dingymist Dorm," I say. "Not our room, of course, but the rest of this place."

"Ha! Dingymist." Sofia laughs. She aims her lens toward our window. "Do something—you can see us in the reflection." I raise one arm in the air and try to lift up a foot with the other. I scrunch my face into a silly pout—mouth closed—and I wait for Sofia to take the photo. "Well, that just looks absurd," she says as our doorbell rings. I drop my foot to the ground and we look at each other questioningly.

"Do you think that's Ella again?" I whisper.

"It has to be, right?" Sofia whispers back, and we both tiptoe—more easily than the first time, now that the floor is clear—over to the door. Sofia peers out the peephole and then nods her head. She unlatches the lock and opens the door. "Hi, Ella, what's . . ." Sofia cuts herself off. I glance over her shoulder to see what she's looking at, and as promised, Ella is there in the hallway.

Only this time, she isn't alone.

"Hi, Avalon and Sofia!" she chirps. "I'm happy to introduce you to your new roommate!"

CHAPTER 8

Sofia and I stand in the doorway in stark silence, dumbstruck. *What does Ella mean, "new roommate"? It's two people per room, and this one is ours.*

"This is Kensington," Ella continues, and if she's picking up any sort of reluctance from Sofia and me, she's choosing to ignore it. "Kensington Barrett."

"Hi," I say shyly.

"Hi there," Sofia says in what I can tell is her trying-to-be-nice voice. "Do you go by Kensington, or a nickname? Kenzie, maybe?"

"Kensington," the girl answers curtly. She has the kind of face that could be pretty . . . if it weren't for its sour expression. Everything else about her is perfectly put together—perfectly highlighted blond hair, perfectly arched eyebrows, perfect dark-wash jeans, perfect black wedges. But her face is so unpleasant-looking that all this perfection is pretty much useless. Perfecto, she is not.

"It seems there was a mix-up with the room assignments," Ella prattles on, oblivious to the tension that has fallen over the space. "And Kensington was given a male roommate—"

"I said that would be fine," Kensington interrupts her.

"It's against the PhotoRetreat rules," Ella fills in. "And, of course, we don't want anyone rooming by themselves—"

"That would also be fine," Kensington interrupts her again.

"Especially for safety reasons," Ella continues, seemingly unperturbed by Kensington's attitude. "So we decided the easiest thing to do was to place both Kensington and her male roommate in preestablished rooms. Oh, here we are—perfecto." I turn toward what Ella is referring to and see two men carrying a bed frame down the hall. Right behind them, two more follow with a bare mattress.

"Where do you want these?" one of the men asks. Ella pushes past us into the bedroom and does a quick sweep with her eyes.

"Wow, you girls have gone to town in here," she says. "Let's place the bed against this wall." She points to the spot in front of our mural—the space where we had mentally placed our phantom beanbag chairs. I glance at Sofia, trying to will her to speak up on our behalf—to say that this is our room, our stuff, our mural wall. But Sofia stays as quiet as I do.

Because, after all, Kensington is standing *right there*.

Looking sour.

The men drag the bed frame and mattress through the door and plop it into place, instantly blocking at least half our pictures.

"Well, I'll leave you three to get acquainted," Ella says cheerily. "Remember, you need to meet the rest of the group in the lobby at four!" I look at my phone screen: 3:14 p.m. We have exactly forty-six minutes—forty-five plus the elevator ride—to waste. If it were just Sofia and me here, the extra time would be welcome—a delay from having to socialize with a bunch of strangers. But now one of those strangers is among us, in our space.

Which makes forty-six minutes seem like an eternity.

Once Ella and the movers have left, Sofia and I look at Kensington expectantly, but she remains eerily quiet, staring ahead out the twinkle light–draped windows.

"So, do you want us to help you bring in your stuff?" I ask, trying to sound friendly.

"This is it," Kensington answers, gesturing to the bag hanging from her shoulder. It's a fairly large bag, but still. Compared to all the stuff Sofia and I brought, it hardly seems like enough.

"That's it?" Sofia asks incredulously. "That's a joke, right?"

"No. Why?" Kensington answers, deadly serious.

"Oh, I just mean, it seems like . . . ," Sofia stutters. "All I'm saying is that if you saw the number of bags Avalon and I arrived with, you would laugh."

"Yes, I gather that," Kensington says, sitting primly on her bare mattress and unzipping her bag. She peers in and pulls out a single flat sheet, followed by a tightly folded blanket and a blow-up pillow, like the kind people use on airplanes.

"Where did you fly here from?" I ask as she begins to drape the sheet over her mattress.

"I'm sorry?"

"The pillow." I point to it.

"Oh," Kensington says. "No, I didn't fly here." When she doesn't elaborate, Sofia and I exchange looks.

Is this girl for real?

"So, where are you from?" Sofia prompts her, as if speaking to a kindergartener.

"Here," Kensington answers.

"Here, like New York?" I ask.

"Yes," Kensington says.

"Wow," Sofia interjects. "That must be so cool." But Kensington only shrugs.

"I mean, it's like being from anywhere else, I guess," she says.

"It's definitely not like being from Arizona," Sofia says, settling cross-legged on her bed. "I've never even been to New York before, and Avalon, you've been here, what did you say, twice?"

"Yeah," I answer. "And only around Christmas."

"Worst time of year," Kensington says. "That's when all the tourists descend."

"Yes, well, I *am* a tourist," I say, maybe a bit too defensively.

"Where are you from?" Kensington asks me. Which I suppose is progress—it is an actual question, after all.

"New Jersey," I tell her. "But South Jersey, closer to Philadelphia."

"Oh" is all Kensington responds. I turn to roll my eyes at Sofia, but she's concentrating on her phone. I climb up the side of our bunk bed to my own mattress and send her a text.

If she lives in New York, why is she staying here?! Go home!

Right????? Sofia responds. *Ugh, so over her. She'll probably tear down our mural while we sleep.*

Before I can reply, a text from Arden appears across my screen. *How's it going?*

I think about how to answer this. If she had asked me an hour ago, I would have said that I was having fun. That I was settling in. That I was . . . happy.

But now? Not so much.

We got a new roommate, I reply.

Wait, what? Who? Arden asks.

Long story, I say, swiping back to the rest of my texts. Where I find six in a row from Celia, all of which I missed while Sofia and I had been decorating our room.

"The key chain!" I call out despite myself.

"What's that?" Sofia asks from her bunk.

"Sorry," I say. "My best friend, she gave me a key chain, and I wanted to put our room key on it."

"Did she give you a friendship bracelet too?" Kensington asks in a mocking tone as I climb down the ladder from my bed. When I reach the floor, I look at Sofia, hoping she'll defend me and put this snotty New Yorker in her place. But Sofia only concentrates harder on her phone, leaving me on my own.

"No," I answer Kensington coldly. "Just the key chain." I open our top dresser drawer and retrieve the bag where I placed it, and then I take the key from my back pocket and loop it through the enclosure. I snap a quick picture of it and send it to Celia with the caption, *Sorry, forgot to do this when I arrived.*

I thought you were going to text me as soon as you got there, Celia responds.

I got distracted decorating the room, I tell her. *How are you?*

But fifteen minutes later, even after I can tell she's read it, Celia doesn't respond.

CHAPTER 9

By the time we leave for our early bird dinner, our new roommate is fully unpacked. And it's obvious that she brought nothing but the bare essentials with her: no keepsakes, no momentos, no reminders from home. Perhaps when home is right down the street, you don't need such things?

Or perhaps Kensington is more robot than human. That somehow seems more likely.

The three of us ride the elevator to the lobby in silence, with even the bond that Sofia and I formed seemingly vanished. When my phone buzzes with a text, I'm relieved to have somewhere to place my eyes. *Arrived at Retirement Ranch. Wish me luck with the Pinochle Posse,* from Arden.

Do you think it's too late for me to join you? I write back as the elevator doors open. I follow Kensington and Sofia out to the main lobby, where Ella, perky as ever, is in the middle, trying to gather the group. I stand as far away from her as possible, moving behind two taller people so I'm out of her sight line. My fear is that if she makes eye contact with me, she'll immediately introduce me to someone else. And the last thing I feel like doing right now is making small talk.

In contrast, I see Sofia flitting around the lobby, talking to anyone she encounters, not looking for me once. My stomach sinks—I had figured we would stick together, like how at home, Celia and I always stick together. If I didn't have Sofia, I'd either have to talk to these strangers, or to no one. It's not that I minded people once I knew them—it was the getting to know them that made me feel unsure. I didn't have it in me to walk up to a stranger and strike up a conversation. I always had Celia around for that job, or Arden, or (I had thought) Sofia. On my own, all I wanted to do was slink off to the side of the lobby and stare at my phone.

I make my way toward a corner, glancing around the room to see if there's anyone who looks half as awkward as I feel. But everyone is already talking to one another—if I walk back over now, I will have to insert myself into someone else's conversation, which is even more horrifying than hiding over here by myself.

I look down at my phone again, willing a text to flash across the screen so I can pretend to be busy. When nothing does, I open the camera instead and aim the lens at the larger group. *I photograph what scares me. I photograph the things I scare.* Sofia's words flash across my mind as I press the button, even though she herself is now hidden within this social circle.

"Paparazzi-ing them?" I whip around to find Kensington seated behind me, so deep in the corner that she's nearly invisible.

"Sorry, I—it just—I didn't see you—" I stutter, feeling the need to explain myself, but Kensington holds up her hand to stop me.

"I get it," she says. "I hate this kind of forced socialization as much as it appears you do. Feel free to stand back here and ignore them all with me."

"Thanks," I say. "I just don't want Ella to yell at us for being, you know, antisocial."

"We're socializing," Kensington reasons. "Look at us—socializing. With each other. That's good enough."

I smile tentatively, settling onto the couch next to Kensington. We sit quietly, waiting for our cue that it's time to leave for dinner. And when we see the rest of the group begin to move toward the lobby doors and out onto the sidewalk, we both stand reluctantly. As we make our way outside, I catch a glimpse of Sofia, chattering away ahead of us.

"I dare you to post that," Kensington says suddenly as we trail behind the group.

"I'm sorry?" I ask, wondering if I was starting to hear things.

"The picture you took," Kensington says. "In the lobby. I dare you to post it and caption it *Forced Socialization.*"

I laugh out loud at this, though Kensington doesn't crack a smile.

"Wouldn't they see?" I ask. "I'm assuming they're going to make us all start following everyone else's PhotoReady accounts."

"Even better," Kensington says. "Give them something to talk about."

I consider this. "I don't think I can. But if you want to post it, I'll send it to you. . . ."

"No, it has to be you," Kensington replies. "You look sweeter. They won't expect it coming from you. And make sure to label it with #PhotoRetreat so it appears in that feed."

I continue to walk beside Kensington, considering this, but I don't make a move to post anything.

"Think of it this way," Kensington continues. "You'd be saying what everyone else is thinking."

"They seem to be enjoying themselves." I gesture to the group ahead of us.

"They're not," Kensington says. "It's all an act. Plus, if you post it, that will at least give them something interesting to say to you. Otherwise, you'll be forced to talk about where everyone's from or whatever. Boring."

"You only think it's boring because you're from New York," I point out. "Of course every other place is boring compared to here."

"I'd kill to not be from here, actually," Kensington tells me. "I mean, not literally kill—I'm not as mean as I look—but trust me: It's annoying."

"Why?" I ask, looking up and down the street as we

cross it. Despite the three or four blocks we've walked, I feel like I've had blinders on until this moment. Like Arden said, people come from everywhere to experience New York. Here I am, right in the thick of it, and I've been too distracted with worrying about who I'm going to talk to at dinner to even see it. When it's right there, all around me.

And magnificent.

"For instance, look at the ivy on that building," I say to Kensington. "You've probably never seen that before."

"There's ivy on a ton of brownstones," Kensington says. "It's kind of a thing."

"But have you ever seen it on *this one*?" I ask. "Like, really noticed it?"

Instead of answering, Kensington gives me a half smile—not with teeth or anything, but there's a definite upturn of her lips, which thus far is the closest I've seen her come to not scowling.

"You're a funny one, you know that?" Kensington says.

"And you're not as scary as you look," I tell her honestly, which makes Kensington break into a genuine, completely unexpected laugh. Right before it ends, I manage to whip my phone out quickly enough to snap a photo of her. And the picture proves that my suspicions about Kensington are correct—that without the sour expression on her face, she really is pretty, with an easy grin that could rival even Arden's.

#IfYouJustSmile, indeed.

"Maybe I'll post this instead," I tell her, holding the photo up for her to see. "You know, I did do my entire PhotoReady project on smiling in order to get in here."

"Of course you did," Kensington says. "And no posting that. You'll damage my street cred." The group in front of us begins to merge through the door of a pizzeria. Before entering, I load the photo I had taken in the dorm lobby onto PhotoReady and give it Kensington's *Forced Socialization* caption, plus the label #PhotoRetreat.

And in the shaded filter that I place over top, the scene doesn't look so frightening after all.

CHAPTER 10

By luck, I end up standing in line at the pizzeria counter next to Sofia, which means I don't have to make small talk with anyone else.

"Where have you been?" Sofia asks as we wait to grab a slice. "I lost you once we got to the lobby."

"I was talking to Kensington," I tell her. "Plus, you looked pretty comfortable making your way through the crowd."

"Kensington?" Sofia asks with wide eyes, ignoring my other comment. "She actually spoke to you?" We each take a slice of pepperoni and head toward two empty seats, Sofia chewing as we walk.

"She's not that bad," I say, looking around to make

sure Kensington can't overhear us. "Really. She just has a very New York personality."

"You mean rude?" Sofia asks. "New Yorkers aren't rude. That's a stereotype."

"I think she's more reserved than rude," I say. "She likes to keep to herself. I don't think that's bad. I kind of do the same thing."

"I do the opposite," Sofia tells me. "I'll talk to anyone, about anything. My family calls it 'word vomit.'"

"Yeah, I noticed," I say with a smile. "But I promise Kensington's better than we thought if you give her a chance."

"Harumph." Sofia makes a grunting sound as she takes another enormous chomp out of her pizza crust. For such a small girl, she sure manages to eat a lot—and quickly. She's already weaving back toward the counter before I'm halfway through my slice. She returns with one for each of us, and I'm certain that a week of eating with her is going to give me indigestion, if nothing else.

"I saw her PhotoReady project," Sofia says after she's swallowed her corner bite.

"Whose?" I ask.

"Kensington's. I looked up her account to find out

what she created to get into the retreat. Guess what the title is?"

"Hold on, I want to see," I say, stuffing the last of my first slice in my mouth so I can retrieve my phone. I open PhotoReady and type "Kensington Barrett" into the search field, but nothing comes up.

"@W84PX," Sofia fills in. "Don't ask me why, but that's her account name."

"How did you ever find her?"

"Please, I can find anyone. It's a gift," Sofia says. "Now look at her project title." I click on one of Kensington's photos—of a gaggle of people hunched over a jewelry case, the surefire signs of visors, sneakers, and large cameras outing them as tourists. The location tag on the photo indicates that it was taken at Tiffany & Co. on Fifth Avenue.

The Tiffany's.

"Wow," I say. "That would be cool to see, huh? I wonder if we'll get to go to Tiffany's this week. Photograph some diamonds."

"You're missing the point—did you see what she labeled her project?" Sofia asks, pointing to Kensington's caption.

"#HometownAttraction?" I ask.

"Yes. It's all pictures of tourists in the city. She's making fun of them."

"I don't think this is making fun of them." I defend Kensington. "She told me that New York can be an annoying place to live sometimes—maybe this is what she meant. That tons of people are always coming here from all over the world, gawking at the place that you think of as yours. I mean, I'd definitely think it was strange if tourists were constantly wandering around my town."

"I think it's snotty," Sofia says. "There, I said it."

"The pictures are nice, though," I say, scrolling through her other shots.

"I'm not impressed," Sofia says.

Before we can continue, one of the PhotoRetreat leaders claps his hands, rising above us as he stands on a chair. I hold out the remainder of my second slice to Sofia, and she consumes the whole thing before he has finished quieting the crowd.

"Do you always eat like this?" I whisper. "It's pretty impressive."

"I ate three Starving Man microwave dinners once. In one sitting," Sofia whispers back.

"Maybe I should have let my mom buy more snacks for our room after all." Sofia gives me a serious nod, and we turn our attention back to the middle of the room.

"For those of you who I haven't met yet, I'm Roberto," the man begins. "I'm an executive at PhotoReady, and this PhotoRetreat was my brainchild."

The room begins applauding Roberto, while Sofia murmurs, "If he does say so himself. . . ."

"As your introductory materials explained, this week is *not* a photography course, per se," Roberto continues. "It's a chance for you—some of our most active junior high school PhotoReady users—to come together, to engage, to start to look at the world around you in a new way. All through, of course, the medium of PhotoReady."

"He's awfully serious," Sofia whispers, and I hit her knee to quiet her.

"Each morning, we'll meet in a makeshift class-room in your dormitory," Roberto continues. "We'll come together to talk about the photos you've taken the day before. In particular, we'll be examining a certain aspect of the pictures, one that will be assigned as you head out for the day. You'll be looking at things like light, contrast, motion. Think of this week as an experiment: a chance to photograph things you've never captured before, and might never get to again. While we hope that by the end, you'll have gathered enough tips and tricks to make your future shots even more successful, the goal here is more about experience than mastery. You have been selected from all corners of the country—learn from each other. See each other. Look at one another—and the city around you—through a brand-new lens."

The room bursts into spontaneous applause again, and Sofia smirks. "How much you want to bet he dreamed of being a poet when he was growing up?" she teases.

"I think it's nice," I tell her. "At least it's not high-pressure."

"Beginning tonight, every time you head out in the city," Roberto continues, "a counselor will be assigned to your group. They will be there to help with directions, to provide guidance, to assist you in finding new subjects to photograph—but only if you need them. If you'd rather explore more independently, the counselors will keep their distance. We understand that for many of you, this will be your first time photographing New York. We encourage you to capture whatever moves you—places, people, scenery, et cetera. Just remember that you're only permitted to use the cameras on your phones—no external equipment—and that no apps besides PhotoReady can be utilized to edit your pictures. By the end of the evening, load your favorite shots onto your profile, and make sure to include the correct label. For this evening, we'll be using #PhotoRetreatNight— since it's your first outing, we're leaving the options open, with your only task being to photograph the city in the evening. Tomorrow morning, we'll take a look at your most interesting shots and discuss them."

One of the retreaters raises his hand. When Roberto points at him, he asks, "Do we have to go as a group, or can we head out by ourselves? I know my way around New York."

"Good question," Roberto says. "You must—*must*— be with at least one other PhotoRetreater at all times, and you must—*must*—be with a counselor as well. While the retreat itself is not meant to be strict, we are rigid on this one point. Got it?" The group nods. "Now starting tomorrow, you can choose your groups yourselves, but tonight, we'd like you to head out with your roommate. It will give you an opportunity to get to know each other before you return to the dorm this evening."

"Wait, that means we have to go with you-know-who," Sofia whispers urgently.

"I told you, she's not bad," I assure her. "But let's hope Ella isn't assigned as our counselor. I don't know if I can take a whole night of 'perfecto' talk."

"Agreed," Sofia nods.

"If you're not already near your roommate, pair off now and start to talk about anything in particular you're hoping to capture. Once a counselor comes your way, you're free to leave."

I glance around the room and catch Kensington's eye. She walks toward us, looking sullen, but I've come to expect that expression from her.

"Be nice," I remind Sofia. "I promise, she's okay."

"I'll believe it when I see it," Sofia says, nevertheless giving Kensington a large fake smile once she reaches us.

"Enjoy your pizza?" she asks her with Ella-level perkiness.

Kensington shrugs and looks to the side. "I thought it was soggy," she says. "The pizza place in my neighborhood is better. This tasted like it came from Long Island. No offense."

"We're not from Long Island," Sofia states defensively. "I don't even know where Long Island is."

"Hi, girls," one of the female counselors approaches us just in time to break up Sofia and Kensington's passive-aggressive pizza fight. "You're the three-peat room, I assume?"

"Not by choice," Sofia mutters under her breath, and I elbow her in the side.

"I'm Nina," the counselor tells us. "If you don't mind, let's exchange cell numbers in case we lose track of each other. Then I'll give you three a chance to discuss where you might want to go tonight—I'm here for directions, or ideas if you need them, but otherwise, you're in charge!"

"We won't need directions," Kensington says shortly, and I catch Sofia rolling her eyes behind her back. Less than five minutes into our first PhotoRetreat mission, and I wasn't sure how we were going to survive the rest of the night together.

Or in this case, the rest of the #PhotoRetreatNight.

CHAPTER 11

Once Nina has our numbers, she leaves us alone to decide where we'd like to go. The three of us stand in a circle, no one saying a word. By this point, the pizzeria is cleared out of PhotoRetreat participants, which means we're behind. And if Sofia and Kensington aren't going to communicate with each other, that only leaves me to speak up, whether I want to or not.

"So," I begin tentatively, "what about Times Square? That has the most lights in the city, right? So it should be pretty easy to photograph at night."

"Yes, I obviously need to see Times Square," Sofia agrees. "Let's go."

"Great," I say, beginning to make my way toward the door.

"You two can't be serious," Kensington says, which makes Sofia cross her arms. "Times Square? There's no way I'm going to Times Square."

"Just because you get to see it every day doesn't mean I have *ever* seen it," Sofia insists. "It's not fair for you to be snobby about it."

"I haven't been to Times Square since like 2009," Kensington argues. "No one from the city ever goes to Times Square."

"Why are you on this retreat anyway, if you're already the New York City expert?" Sofia asks. "What's the point?"

I feel my face growing hot with embarrassment—even if I'm not directly involved in this fight, it's uncomfortable enough to watch. But Kensington only gives Sofia a long, dismissive sigh. "Look," she begins. "Either we go to Times Square, like everyone else at this retreat—and everyone else in the world, for that matter—because that's the only place they've ever heard of. Or you can trust me to show you the places the tourists don't see. The real New York."

I look at Sofia, trying to will her to agree. It's not that I wouldn't like to see Times Square again, but Kensington has a point. What's the use of having a real New York native with you if you're just going to go to all the tourist traps? If we follow Kensington's lead, we might be able to capture more interesting scenes than the chaotic hustle of Times Square.

That is, if she and Sofia don't strangle each other in the meantime.

When Sofia remains silent, I suggest a compromise. "How about tonight, Kensington leads the way, and we try to go to Times Square at some other point this week?"

"Fine," Sofia agrees more quickly than I had assumed she would. "But I need to see Times Square before we leave."

I ignore the face Kensington makes out of Sofia's view as I guide them toward the pizzeria's door. "So, Kensington, you're in charge." Kensington passes in front of me, tossing her blond hair off one of her shoulders before coming to a short stop.

"Wait, before we leave, tell me what you'd like to do tonight. I'm not talking about pictures. I'm talking about *doing*," Kensington says.

"Eat," Sofia answers almost instantly, which makes me laugh.

"I'm with her," I say.

"What, specifically, would you like to eat?" Kensington asks. "This will help narrow down where we go."

"Dessert," Sofia and I answer at the same time, and now it's Sofia's turn to laugh.

"Cupcakes or cookies or ice cream or what?" Kensington asks. "I need particulars."

"Your choice," I say to Sofia. "I would eat any of them."

"Cookies," Sofia says. "Definitely cookies."

"Got it," Kensington says, pushing through the door. "Nina, we're headed to the Upper West Side." Kensington begins walking with purpose down the sidewalk, Sofia and I scrambling to stay near her. And while I try to keep my eyes peeled for good photographs, I'm distracted by the looks on both Sofia's and Kensington's faces. Where there at the bottom, right below their noses, are the smallest, faintest traces of honest-to-goodness smiles.

Within a few minutes, I find myself doing something I've never experienced before: riding the subway.

Kensington helps Sofia and me buy MetroCards, and she shows us how to swipe them at the turnstiles in order to reach the train platform. I don't think we're doing much to convince her we're not the country bumpkins she thinks we are, but I barely care anymore. It somehow feels right to have Kensington as the boss, and despite the number of new experiences—and new people—all around me, I feel safe with her around. Kensington doesn't look like the type of person who takes any nonsense, from strangers or otherwise.

In contrast, I'm pretty sure that Sofia and I look wide-eyed and innocent enough to be the target of anything New York has to offer.

As the train pulls into the station, I turn and see Nina standing a respectful twenty feet behind us. She boards the same subway car but remains at the other end of it.

"It's like we have our own Secret Service agent," I say as the three of us huddle around a pole, holding on.

"I know," Sofia agrees. "I kind of feel sorry for Nina— do you think we should include her?"

"No," Kensington answers definitively.

"Are you sure?" I ask. "It seems impolite to ignore her."

Kensington sighs, as if we're exhausting her. "If we

include Nina, she's going to start thinking she has a say in where we go," she explains. "These college kids, they come to the city and suddenly think they're experts on the place. Trust me, Avalon Kelly, we don't want her interfering." I begin to respond but then snap my mouth closed in surprise—how did Kensington know my last name? I'm sure I never told her . . . maybe Ella did? Was it somewhere on our dorm materials?

"How do you know her name?" Sofia asks before I think of a way to broach the subject. So much for subtlety.

"I saw it on PhotoReady, Sofia Aronzo," Kensington answers. "You're not the only one who can properly track down people on the Internet." I'm afraid this exchange is going to turn into another battle between them, but instead, Sofia looks impressed.

And maybe even entertained.

Could Room 609 maybe, possibly, be starting to gel?

"Then why didn't you follow our accounts, once you found us? Huh?" Sofia asks in a teasing tone. "Too good for us?"

"The same reason you didn't follow me when you found my profile, I'd imagine," Kensington answers. "Following first is essentially showing the other person that you cared enough to search for them. I didn't want to give you the satisfaction."

"Okay, can we please all follow each other now, and get it over with?" I interject. The three of us pull out our phones and open PhotoReady as the train comes to a halt. I look out the door and see a sign that reads *Times Square—42 Street*.

"Hey, Sofia," I say, pointing. "Look where we are."

"Don't get too excited," Kensington says. "We're not getting off. Though the good news is this station has cell service, so we can get this you-follow-me-I'll-follow-you ridiculousness completed."

"What's your PhotoReady name again?" I ask her.

"@W84PX," she tells us.

"You know you're going to have to explain that one, right?" Sofia says.

"It's part of the street address for Kensington Palace in London," she answers. "Not all of us are so literal as to put our actual names in our actual profiles, @SofiaNoPH and @AvalonByTheC."

"Very funny," I say. "Hey, do you think I could take some pictures while we're on here, or will people beat me up?" I ask Kensington quietly, looking around.

There are some great characters in this subway car that I'd love to capture. Specifically the man carrying an antique birdcage with nothing but crinkled tutus inside.

"I wouldn't do it," she says. "But if you want to take a picture of *us*, no one will stop you."

"You're going to let me take your picture?" I ask, mocking a shocked expression as I flip my lens around for a selfie. The three of us squeeze our heads into the frame, and Sofia calls, "Cheese!" as I snap the photo. I take down my phone so we can examine ourselves.

"That's definitely post-worthy," Sofia decides.

"Agreed," Kensington says. When they both look away, back to their own phones, I load the picture onto PhotoReady, cropping myself—and my metal smile— out of it. Sofia's and Kensington's heads fill the frame, genuinely happy grins on each of their faces. *Subway smiling,* I caption the photo, then I give it the correct #PhotoRetreatNight label.

"Here we are," Kensington says as I feel the train coming to a stop. She pushes off the subway as the doors open, dragging Sofia by the wrist while Sofia drags me. We step onto the platform and I look at the sign above us: *66th Street—Lincoln Center*. Over sixty blocks from where we were minutes ago, and a world away from where I started this morning.

CHAPTER 12

Sofia and I follow Kensington as she leads us down one flight of stairs then back up another, down a corridor and through a bright underground hallway.

"Do you get the feeling that we're the rats, and she's the Pied Piper?" I remark as we scramble to keep up with her. Even with the chunky wedges on her shoes, Kensington somehow manages to outpace Sofia and me by at least three strides at all times.

"Please don't mention rats while we're in the subway," Sofia tells me.

"I don't think rats actually live down here," I say. "At least not that we would see. That's probably an urban myth."

"Oh, no—it's true," Kensington calls back. "Take a good look at the tracks when we're headed downtown later. You'll most likely spot one scampering across."

I see Sofia do a full-body shiver at this news as we step onto an up escalator.

"Where are you taking us?" Sofia asks, as I turn and see Nina boarding the escalator behind us. I wonder if we're the group that has traveled farthest from the dorm—and whether Nina loves us for it, or hates us.

"I figured to appease you, I'd give you a touch of tourist first," Kensington says as she reaches the top of the escalator, Sofia and I on her heels. "Ta-da." She says this last part in her typically unenthused tone, which makes it all the funnier.

"Wow, Carnegie Hall?" Sofia asks.

"Lincoln Center," I correct her, gazing around at the trio of white buildings as we make our way toward the center of the plaza. A gigantic round fountain sits in the middle, spewing water up toward the sky at select intervals. My family and I had come here to see *The Nutcracker* when I was younger, but that was in the middle of the day. At dusk, the place looks much more magical.

"Hurry up and take your tourist shots so I can show you the more exciting part," Kensington says, and dutifully, Sofia and I whip out our phones and begin photographing the place from all angles.

The three of us run off in different directions—well, Sofia and I run; Kensington saunters—each trying to capture the scene from a new perspective. I head to the sidewalk to photograph the stairs leading to the plaza. When I lean all the way down and place my camera along the top of a step, I manage to fit the stairs, fountain, and front of the Metropolitan Opera House all in the same frame. I trot back up the stairs, snapping pictures of the square edges leading to the Philharmonic's entrance, then I scurry over and stand on a ledge to the right of the opera house, leaning back to photograph the humongous arches of its façade. From this perch, I look around for my people. I spot Nina near the escalator where we got off, trying to keep an eye on all of us at once. Sofia has seated herself on the rim around the fountain, taking selfies with the shooting water as a backdrop. And even Kensington is taking pictures—granted, she's practically sitting on the ground, seemingly photographing a stray ant, but still. I would have expected her to be standing off in the corner mocking us for being touristy.

I jump off the ledge and skip over, startling her from behind. "Look who's actually being a tourist," I tease her.

"Not a tourist," Kensington says, rising to her feet and dusting off her knees. "I was taking pictures of you two frolicking around. Look." She holds out her phone, and I see a photo of Sofia leaning on the fountain, trying to pose like she's a 1950s calendar girl, but with her phone blocking her entire face. "Come on, that's brilliant."

"It's pretty good," I say. "Should we load our favorites while we wait for her to finish modeling?"

"I suppose," Kensington says, and we both get to work on PhotoReady. I don't want to overdo it, so I choose one of my step pictures, and another of the Metropolitan Opera House's arches, placing a shadowy filter over each to bring out their moody light.

"New York is awesome!" Sofia appears next to us, saying each word like it has an exclamation point after it.

"You ain't seen nothin' yet," Kensington says, gesturing for us to follow her as she heads off the plaza. She leads us past a pool of shallow water with two sculptures resting in the center, and we pass a restaurant with dressed-up people sitting at tables outside.

"Do you think we could stop here for a snack?" Sofia calls after Kensington.

"You can't possibly be hungry already," I comment.

Sofia gives me an innocent look as Kensington whirls around. "Do you have a tapeworm?" she asks. "Come see this, and then I'll take you for the best cookie of your life."

"Ooh, let's speed it up, then," Sofia says, beginning to jog in order to keep up with Kensington's gait. At the corner of the restaurant, Kensington turns right and starts stomping across a grassy lawn, up and up, toward another corner of the building.

Only it's not a lawn at all—the entire roof of the restaurant has been turned into a miniature park, with groups of people sprinkled around it, sitting and talking with one another. The entire thing sits at a diagonal, so the grass slopes up in two of its corners, as if you're climbing hills in the middle of a pasture.

"I feel like I'm in *The Sound of Music*," Sofia says as she spins around, arms outstretched on either side of her. I snap a picture as she twirls, and I load it onto Photo-Ready, captioning it *The hills are alive* and giving it the correct label. Meanwhile, Kensington strolls to the other high corner of the lawn to take pictures of the plaza from afar, Sofia and I scampering after her.

"Have I mentioned I love New York?" Sofia asks, flopping down on her back and waving her arms and legs back and forth as if she's creating a snow angel.

"How do you know about snow angels?" I ask her. "Have you ever had one flake of snow in Arizona?" Sofia leans up on one elbow to face me.

"Sand angels," she says seriously. "Don't knock it till you've tried it!"

I sit next to her, and she holds her phone out in front of our faces. "Let's take a picture of us in nature," she suggests. We lean our heads together, and Sofia snaps the photo just as Kensington inserts herself in the frame, making a face behind our heads. When Sofia opens the photo so we can examine our work, the three of us—Kensington, too—collapse into a fit of giggles. The kind of giggles so uncontrollable that if we were in class right now, we would almost certainly get written up by the teacher, yet we still wouldn't be able to stop them.

"Don't you dare load that, Arizona," Kensington tells her. "I can't have those kinds of pictures of me floating around on the interwebs."

"I agree," I say, rising to stand. "Let's keep that one for our own amusement."

"Ugh, fine," Sofia says, and I'm grateful that together, Kensington and I have some semblance of power over Sofia's lightning-quick posting finger.

"Let's go, tourists," Kensington says, pretending to haul us up by our armpits. "Time to get this one a cookie before she faints from hunger."

"Just when I thought this day couldn't get any better!" Sofia exclaims, jumping up in the air and clicking her heels together.

"Wait, do that again," I instruct. "And Kensington, do it with her. But face the corner, so that the buildings are behind you."

"You're quite the demanding photo director, Avalon Kelly," Kensington says, but they listen to me anyway, clicking their heels together repeatedly until the right image is captured.

The image—just possibly—of a brand-new friendship.

After we leave Lincoln Center, Kensington leads us through the Upper West Side all the way to Seventy-Fourth Street. She makes a sharp turn to head down a small flight of stairs (if there's anything I've learned from following her around all evening, it's that besides walking faster than anyone on the planet, she also never indicates what direction she's going before making the turn). A deep, luscious scent soon envelops my senses: the smell of sugar and chocolate and freshly brewed coffee.

"I am never leaving this place," Sofia calls, barreling ahead of me down the rest of the stairs and into Levain Bakery.

"Well, they close in five minutes, so unless you want to get locked in here all night . . . ," Kensington begins.

"There are worse things," Sofia insists. "Oh, for the love . . . Will you look at these cookies!"

"Yes, you're welcome," Kensington says. "They're about to change your life."

The three of us each pay for one chocolate chip walnut cookie (my suggestion that we share one, since the cookies are roughly the size of my head, was quickly shot down by Sofia). Reluctantly, we leave the scent of Levain behind us as we reemerge onto the sidewalk. I take a bite out of this massive hunk of baked dough, and I realize immediately that Kensington is right—these cookies are unreal. Life-changing, even. Crispy on the outside, chewy on the inside, and they are warm enough that the chocolate melts on my face as I make my way toward the center.

"I'm never going to be able to eat another cookie again," Sofia says. "This thing is out of this world."

"Told you," Kensington says with a flick of her hair. "Come on—walk and eat at the same time. I want to show you something else before it's closed." I take advantage of a red light to photograph the giant cookie in my palm, a taxicab rushing by at exactly the right moment to create a blur of yellow in the background. I then wrap up the rest and deposit it in my bag, since there's no way I'd be able to finish the whole thing right now (I figure this is also a good move before Sofia the bottomless pit volunteers to polish off the rest for me).

"Here we are," Kensington announces a few blocks later, coming to a harsh stop outside a tall, black prison-like gate.

"Septuo-gee . . . ," Sofia tries to read the sign hanging on the outside of the fence. "Sorry, this is Super-calafragilistic territory."

Septuagesimo Uno, I read, though I have no idea how to pronounce it either. "What is it?" I ask Kensington, looking through the grates. It's hard to see in the dim light, but I make out a brick path and a couple of benches, with some scattered bushes and flowers in between.

"The smallest park in New York," Kensington answers.

"Seriously?" Sofia asks as Kensington pushes through the gate and walks inside. "This is considered a park? It's more like an alley. With trees."

"Still a park," Kensington says. We walk to the back of the space—which only takes a few large steps, based on the size—and I look up. Two brownstones form the sides of the park, and Sofia is right—without the trees and benches and brick pathway, it really wouldn't be much more than an alley. But with them, the place is charming, quiet, a kind of escape from the rest of the city. And after only a few hours "living" here, I can already see how such qualities would be important.

"See, the real tourists, they go to Central Park. But you guys get the smallest park in New York City," Kensington says, lowering herself onto a bench. "How many people in New Jersey and Arizona can say they've been here?"

"Very true," I agree, trying to photograph my

surroundings, but it's hard to see anything. I flip on the flash and try again.

"Oh no, no, no," Kensington says. "Cardinal rule of PhotoReady—no flash."

"Right," Sofia says. "Flashes completely wash me out."

"You're not even in this picture," I say. "And it's too dark here to take anything without the flash. It doesn't show up well."

"Then we'll be your lights," Sofia volunteers. "You go high, I'll go low." She says this last part to Kensington. The two of them turn on their phones so that the brightness of their screens can serve as my lighting. Kensington holds hers above my head, and Sofia poses at my knees.

"You two might be geniuses, you know that?" I say, turning in a circle to try to capture the entire space at once. "Got it," I tell them once I'm satisfied. "I'm going to caption this *Good things come in small packages.*"

"Perfect," Kensington says, marching back to the gate, Sofia and I falling in line behind her.

"That's quite the compliment coming from you," I tell her.

"What did you expect me to say?" she asks, shutting the gate behind us. "Perfecto?"

CHAPTER 13

Nina is standing next to the Septuagesimo Uno gate when we exit, waiting for us. "I wanted to give you girls a heads-up that we're going to have to start back in the next twenty minutes or so. We have an eight thirty p.m. curfew."

"Whoa, it's been almost three hours already?" Sofia asks, glancing at the time on her phone screen.

"Time flies when you're having fun," I agree, surprised to find that I *am* having fun. Much more than I ever thought I would.

"One more place," Kensington insists. "Then I promise I'll get us back in time. Move it or lose it." Kensington makes a left and walks full-steam ahead down the block—faster than she has walked all night, which is really saying something.

"What is it?" I call after her, trying not to sound winded as we fly across West End Avenue and make a right, and then another left on Seventy-Second Street.

"Have I led you astray yet, Avalon Kelly?" Kensington responds.

"Are you always going to call me by my full name, Kensington Barrett?" I ask her.

"It's got a ring to it," she says. "And don't copycat me." We zoom across the street again as the light turns red, and then across another.

"Who's that a statue of?" Sofia tries to ask Kensington as we pass it, but Kensington only waves her arms dismissively.

"Eleanor Roosevelt, but no time for her right now," she says. I try to snap a photo of the statue anyway, which puts me a few paces behind. We're nearly jogging as we pass a dog run on the left, and then dart through a small tunnel. Kensington comes to a sudden halt—once again, I've come to learn this is her specialty—along a stone wall on the other side, and she places both arms out in front of her, as if balancing a tray.

"I present your home state, Avalon Kelly," she says. I look to where she's pointing, and there, through some tree branches and across the water, I see lights lining the other side of the Hudson River. New Jersey. Home. It's nowhere near the level of the New York City skyline, but it's there, shining, all the same.

And somehow the mere sight of it, even from miles and a body of water away, makes me smile. A real smile. With teeth and everything.

Lying in my bunk that night, only the glow of the twinkle lights piercing through the darkness, I try to force myself to fall asleep. I look around for a clock so I can mentally calculate how much rest I'll get before we have to wake up for our group photo discussion, but neither Sofia nor I brought one, and Kensington, with her minimalist packing technique, certainly wouldn't have had one in her Mary Poppins–type bag. I had plugged my phone into the outlet next to the printer so that it could get a full charge overnight, which I now realize was a mistake. Because not only do I not know what time it is, but I have nothing with which to entertain myself while I wait for some form of drowsiness to hit.

I rearrange myself in bed, trying to keep the squeaking of the coils beneath my mattress to a minimum so as to not disturb Sofia. But the room is so silent, with only the faintest hint of deep breathing, that it appears my roommates are already asleep. I look over the side of my bed and try to make Kensington's form out of the shadows of the twinkle lights, but it's too dark to see. I flip around again and try lying on my back, staring at the ceiling. I would give almost anything to be home in my own bed right now. Not even because I'm having a bad time—the day was about one thousand percent more enjoyable than I had anticipated—but because I know I can sleep there. And nothing makes you homesick faster than a bed that keeps you awake.

I try to lull myself to sleep, pretending the sounds of traffic outside the windows are soothing instead of distracting, but nothing seems to work. I sit up in bed, careful to do so slowly so that I don't smack my head against the ceiling, and I look across the room toward my phone. Should I risk waking the roommates? Should I risk knocking myself unconscious by climbing down this bunk bed's ladder with little more than twinkle lights to guide me?

Yes.

As carefully as possible, I maneuver myself to the foot of my bed, and I slide, snake-style, off the side until my foot hits a rung of the ladder. I lower myself to the floor, mentally congratulating myself for being so silent and stealth. Maybe I had more ninja qualities than I initially thought. Perhaps all those years of watching Jelly gracefully leap from one piece of furniture to the next had taught me how to—

"Ow! Oof! No! Ow!"

The form that is Kensington sits up straight in her bed, which I have apparently stubbed my toe into the side of.

"Weak bladder?" she whispers to me.

"Very funny," I say. "I can't sleep and I want my phone."

"The first step of addiction is admitting you have a problem," she says in hushed tones, but even without being able to fully see her face, I can tell that she's smirking.

"Huh?" I manage to make it the rest of the way across the room and take my phone off its charger, using its lighted screen to help me return. With the amount of stuff Sofia and I had jammed into this space, not to mention the whole additional person, it was a minefield to make it from one side of the room to the other.

"You're addicted to your phone," Kensington says. "If you need it to sleep."

"I don't need it to sleep. I can't sleep, so I want something to do," I explain.

"Essentially the same thing. But now that you have me up, I might as well go to the bathroom."

"Who has the weak bladder now?" I tease her, beginning to climb up to my bunk. On the way, I use the light of my phone to check on Sofia, but she is still fast asleep, her face mostly buried under her blanket. I reach the top of the ladder and crawl across my mattress, settling in with my phone and feeling much better than I did a few minutes ago.

Which means maybe Kensington is right. Maybe this thing is like my security object. . . .

Oh, well. There are worse things.

I open PhotoReady and find at least triple the number of notifications as usual, many of them from usernames I don't recognize.

"Hey," I whisper to Kensington once she returns. "Did a bunch of random people star your photos from today?"

"I don't know because my phone isn't attached to my

body at all times," she says. "But it's most likely the other retreat people. Don't get too big a head." She smacks her inflatable airplane pillow against my face.

"If Sofia weren't asleep right now, I'd get you for that," I tell her.

"Sure, you're really a fierce opponent when it takes you half the night to get up and down that ladder," Kensington retorts.

"What is with that pillow, anyway?" I ask. "You couldn't carry a real pillow all the way down the street?"

"I don't like to overpack," Kensington says. "A sentiment I see you and the other hoarder on the bottom bunk do not share."

"Very funny," I say. "Is the light from my phone going to bother you?"

"Not any more than these Christmas tree lights," Kensington answers. "Good night."

"Night." I shimmy further under my blanket, turning back to the PhotoReady notification list. About half are from people I know, and the other half strangers.

But not a single star from Celia.

I switch over to my texts and look at our chain again. She still hasn't responded to my last message. She can't be mad at me, can she? I mean, she's the one who told me to go on the retreat. She pretty much insisted. So now, why is she being weird?

You up? I type to her, and I wait for my phone to buzz back. I send the same note to Arden, but she's quiet too. I wish for a moment that Jelly had a cell phone—or, maybe more important, an ability to use it—so I could text her, and then I smile to myself imagining how Kensington would react if I expressed this thought out loud. Just as I'm about to turn off my phone and give up, the screen lights up with a text from Celia.

Yes, is all she writes.

Thank goodness!!! I can't sleep. Why didn't you answer me before? I ask.

A few seconds later, she replies, *Seemed like you were busy with your new BFF.* And before I can respond, she adds, *Actually, make that BFFs. Multiple.*

I feel my face flush with warmth, flashing back to Sofia's caption from earlier in the day. *Come on, you know you can't take that seriously,* I assure Celia. *So how are you?*

You said you were going to text me, Celia replies, ignoring my question. *You promised you wouldn't forget about me.*

I HAVEN'T forgotten about you! I'm texting you now, aren't I?

Celia is quiet, and for a moment I fear she's ignoring me again. *How's NJ?* I prompt her, trying to force our conversation back to normal.

It's fine, she replies. *So you like the retreat?*

More than I thought I would, I tell her honestly. *But I wish you were here.*

Call me tomorrow, Celia requests. *Please? I want to know what's going on, and not just through dumb Sofia's PhotoReady stream.*

I will, I promise.

"Okay, I take it back," Kensington whisper-yells across the room. "The light doesn't bother me, but do you need to have the keyboard sound turned on so I hear every single letter you type?"

"Sorry, Sleeping Beauty," I tease her. I jam my phone underneath my pillow, flip myself over, and lie on my stomach, my face turned toward the wall.

And despite everything, namely my fears that I never would, I eventually fall asleep.

CHAPTER 14

The following morning, the three of us sit in a row in the middle of the PhotoRetreat makeshift classroom in the basement of Dingymist Dorm. Sofia is chomping through the last of a blueberry muffin—I stopped counting after her second pastry and third plate of fruit—while Kensington and I watch her, fascinated.

"*Where* do you put it all?" Kensington asks. "Seriously, have you ever been checked for parasites?"

Sofia shrugs. "Don't be a metabolism hater," she says as Roberto strolls to the front of the room. He hits a few buttons on his tablet until the large screen at the front comes to life, a slew of pictures filling the frame from one end to the other. I recognize a couple of my own shots, and the sight of them in such a large format makes my stomach start to feel as knotty as it did in the car yesterday.

"How long is this supposed to last?" I whisper to Sofia and Kensington.

"Whatever it is, it's too long," Kensington answers. "I'm bored already."

"Isn't this why we came here?" Sofia asks. "To learn how to take better pictures?"

"I thought we came to photograph New York," I say. "Which doesn't explain what *you're* doing here." I nudge Kensington's elbow off her armrest, and she shoves mine back.

"Okay, then," Roberto begins. I turn and see the counselors assembled in the chairs on the side of the room, waiting. Ella is sitting up straight, her hands folded on the desk ledge in front of her. The model student. Naturally. "Now, last night was a free-form outing, where you could photograph anything that captured your eye, with little direction from us. Earlier today, I went through the shots with the #PhotoRetreatNight tag and chose some for us to discuss. Take a look at the collage on the screen, and make a note of those photos you admire, or are intrigued by, or think could be improved in some way. Feedback doesn't have to be positive, but it must be constructive. I'll give you a few moments to peruse them."

I examine the board, squirming in my seat and hoping that I can make it through the class without my photos—or me—being singled out. "Participation" has never exactly been my strong suit in school—I always preferred to sit back, to stay below the radar, to not be acknowledged, at least not publicly. It's not that I wasn't interested in hearing what others had to say—I just wasn't interested in hearing what they had to say about *my* pictures. Especially if what they had to say was negative.

"Who would like to begin?" Roberto asks entirely too quickly. "Yes, in the corner." He points to the far side of the room as I drum my fingers against my thigh, nervous.

The hand raiser requests Roberto to zoom in on a picture in the center of the screen. "The arch from Washington Square Park," she begins. "From the angle it was shot, you wouldn't know if it was taken in New York or Paris. But the one person in the corner gives it away with the *I Heart NY* T-shirt." It's definitely a pretty shot, but I never would have noticed the person in the New York shirt if it weren't pointed out to me. Maybe

I'm not observant enough to think like a real photographer. Or even a real wannabe photographer.

My thoughts are disturbed by my phone buzzing in my pocket, and I reach for it, seeing Celia's face pop up on my screen, calling me. I quickly press decline and then send her a text: *Can't talk now*. When I manage to focus again, I see Roberto has switched to a new image. This one appears to have been taken on a corner, facing the buildings across the street.

"I feel as though this perfectly captures the rule of thirds," one of the other retreaters is saying. "If you draw four lines across it—two horizontal and two vertical—the main focal points would fall at the intersections."

"*What* is he talking about?" I whisper to Kensington.

"Just being pretentious," Kensington answers. "Trying to show off what he knows. It's like Photography by Wikipedia." I have to bite the insides of my mouth to keep from giggling at this, and I turn back to my phone and open PhotoReady, finding a new slew of notifications. A profile with the name @TaterTotter has starred every single one of my photos from last night, including the *Forced Socialization* one. I look at the pictures in @TaterTotter's stream, trying to figure out who this person is. There are only three photos from last night, but they are more interesting to me than most of the snapshots I've seen Roberto highlight so far. A silhouette of a woman walking her dog—or really, being pulled by her dog, despite its miniature size—up a brownstone stoop. A busy crosswalk as taken through a hole in a broken fence. A police officer gazing down the street in the direction of a horse-drawn carriage, but the angle makes it look like the horse is charging him.

And even though I don't feel like I know much about photography, other than saying which pictures I like or don't, I'm drawn to these. They tell a story. There's life behind them.

I'm so distracted by @TaterTotter's stream that I don't notice at first when Roberto clicks on one of my photos, enlarging it across the screen, until Sofia and Kensington begin hitting my knees.

"That's from the tiny park!" Sofia whispers excitedly. I do a sweep of the room with my eyes, looking for the person who requested it, all without moving my head so that no one can guess the photo belongs to me.

"I like the light in this one," I hear a voice from across the room, and I turn to see where it's coming from (which is safe to do only because everyone else is turning as well). "I always have trouble taking pictures at night, and this place somehow seems naturally lit, even though it's dark outside." The face of the speaker is blocked by those sitting around him, so all I can tell is that a) it's a boy, and b) well, that's about it.

"Nice feedback," Roberto says. "I agree about the light—it's almost as if it's being provided by the moon itself, which is a cool thought. The idea that the moonlight could reach this small, alley-like space, and brighten it." Kensington and Sofia turn to me with raised eyebrows, seemingly impressed that Roberto, who hasn't been all that complimentary thus far, likes my shot. For a moment, the jumping jacks inside my stomach cease, and I feel mildly proud of myself. But then Roberto continues, "Who can take credit for this picture?"

And the jumping jacks return, stronger than ever.

I sit absolutely still, as if my arms have been papier-mâchéd against my body.

"Raise your hand!" Sofia hisses, and it feels like it takes every muscle in my body to lift my right arm into the air.

"Name?" Roberto asks me. Has he been doing this to

everyone whose photos were highlighted? I really should be paying more attention.

"Avalon Kelly," I say without too much stammering.

"No, PhotoReady name," he corrects me.

"Oh, sorry. @AvalonByTheC. But, like, with the letter C. Instead of the ocean 'sea,'" I explain. I'm babbling.

"Very good," Roberto says. "Who else sees a photo that struck them in some way?"

Even with the focus off me again, I can't seem to stop my heart from beating ferociously in the back of my neck, pounding against my throat. When the rest of the room seems otherwise engaged examining a new picture, I turn slowly over my shoulder, searching for the person who singled out my photo. I look in the direction where the voice had come, but the only boy sitting in that corner has a bright green scarf wrapped around his neck, shielding his profile. I lean forward slightly to get a better look, and his face comes into view.

And it is a face I somehow recognize.

He catches my eye before I can place him, and I snap my head back to the front, a deep flush of heat filling my cheeks. Why does he look familiar? Did I see him in the dorm lobby? Or at the pizzeria? That has to be it . . . right?

I tap my foot against the ground in bursts of manic staccatos until Kensington slaps my leg down with a *thwap*. "Sit still. You're giving me anxiety," she whispers.

Who is *he?*

I turn on my phone again, and the last thing I was looking at appears on my screen: @TaterTotter's PhotoReady page. I'm about to close it and check my newest notifications when I spot it. Well, not so much "it" as "him."

At the top of @TaterTotter's page, I see the face in the profile picture—the face from the corner of the room, including the same green scarf. Very carefully, I look over my shoulder to be sure, and @TaterTotter himself is staring back at me. When he sees me turn to face him, he breaks into an enormous grin.

And it's no exaggeration when I say that it may very well be an even better grin than Arden's, or Kensington's, or anyone else who has smiled—ever—in life.

CHAPTER 15

"Who're you stalking there?" Kensington startles me to the point that I nearly drop my phone on the floor.

I look at Roberto, who is leading a discussion about another photo, and I send her a text instead of replying out loud.

The guy who said he liked my picture, I type, and I watch Kensington read it.

Tate? she writes back.

? I don't know his name.

It's Tate, Kensington answers. *He was the roommate I was initially assigned to. You know, when they thought I was a boy.*

Ha. His PhotoReady name is @TaterTotter.

I'm sure you think that's adorable. I'll introduce you after this joy is over.

Nooooooo, so embarrassing! Don't you dare!

Well, now I'm definitely going to, she says. *You pretty much cemented your fate.*

I send back an angry face, followed by, *I don't like to meet new people.*

That would explain your "welcoming" reaction to me, Kensington writes, and I have to laugh.

He looks much older than us, right? I ask about Tate.

Speak for yourself.

No, but really, I continue. *He looks like he's in high school.*

He's in eighth grade, so a year older? Kensington writes. *He lives somewhere near Boston. And that's all the info I got before they realized I wasn't a boy.*

I sense movement around the room and lift my head to see people rising from their seats. "What's going on?" I ask Sofia.

"Roberto is giving us a ten-minute break," she says. "Have you two listened to a single word today?"

"This one blanked out after she realized she had a

fan," Kensington answers. "Come on, I'll introduce you. You should come too, Short Stack."

"Am I supposed to be Short Stack?" Sofia asks her.

"Well, you are short, and I assume you can eat multiple pancake stacks in record time, so yes," Kensington replies.

"Okay, that's valid," Sofia says, and she follows as Kensington drags me—truly drags me—across the room.

"Tate!" Kensington calls when we're still at least ten feet away from him. I immediately stand up straight and try to look normal, rather than like a toddler who is being pulled across the room against her will. And I swear, something about the way he turns makes it look like he's moving in slow motion, like I have many minutes to prepare myself for the face-to-face encounter instead of the half a second it actually takes. I want to lower my eyes, to not witness his reaction to this all-but-certainly awkward introduction, but I also can't seem to look away.

"Hey, Kenz," he says.

Kenz?

"Kenz?" Sofia says out loud, echoing my thoughts. "Didn't she shoot down all nicknames within moments of meeting us?"

Kensington ignores her. "Hey, roomie," she greets him, casually friendly, and very unlike the Kensington who was dumped on our doorstep yesterday. How long, exactly, did it take for the PhotoRetreat people to realize Kensington wasn't a boy before they broke these two up? Because they seem awfully chummy.

"Excuse you, *we're* your roomies," Sofia interjects, followed immediately by, "Hi, I'm Sofia." She extends her hand to shake Tate's.

"Charmed," Tate responds. *Charmed?* "And I recognize @AvalonByTheC here."

I open my mouth to speak, but that familiar pounding is back against my throat, rendering my vocal cords useless.

"Yeah, way to make the rest of us look bad by going on and on about her brilliance," Kensington says, teasing him.

"Sorry, Kenz, but I have to acknowledge greatness when I see it," Tate says. "And not everyone can convince the moon to shine specifically in the darkest alley of Manhattan, all for the benefit of a single picture."

I blink rapidly and clear my throat, willing my voice to work again so as to not look like a moron. But Sofia beats me to the punch.

"It was us, you know," she says. "Kensington and I lit the space with our phones—she held hers at the top, and I—"

"Way to steal the thunder, Short Stack," Kensington interrupts her. It's again in her teasing tone, but there's slightly more harshness to it. "I'm going to run to the restroom—do you know where it is?"

"Oh yeah, I saw it when we came in. I can show . . . ," I begin, my voice suddenly recovered, and I start to push toward the door.

"I was talking to Shortie Aronzo," Kensington interrupts me. She takes Sofia by the elbow and yanks her toward the door. Right before they step into the hall, she calls over her shoulder, "By the way, she already stalked your PhotoReady page!"

And I swear, if I could locate a fire extinguisher right now, I would use it to put out the blaze on my face. But Tate, to his great credit, only laughs at this news, retrieving his phone from his back pocket. "I assume you found me after I was stalking you?" he asks. "Which would make me the primary stalker."

"Um, yeah," I say, grateful that my voice sounds fairly normal. "I saw you had starred my photos, so I went snooping on your profile." I decide to be honest. "Your pictures are pretty awesome. Not pretty awesome, actually—*definitely* awesome."

"Thank you," Tate replies. "And your *Forced Socialization* picture made me laugh."

"That was Kensington's idea," I tell him. "I mean, I took the picture, but she's the one who told me to post it."

"It was great, even if it was a group effort," Tate says. "So where're you from?"

"New Jersey," I answer, waiting for a Kensington-like dismissive response. After all, if Tate is also from a city, then I'm sure the suburbs of South Jersey seem as boring to him as they do to my loudmouth roommate. He'll probably lose interest in this entire conversation immediately, and my pictures won't seem so "interesting" anymore.

"Oh, excellent," Tate responds. "I assume that explains your name?"

"You know Avalon?" I ask. "Kensington told me you were from Boston."

"So you already asked about me, huh?" Tate says, a slight smile appearing on his lips. "I'm kidding you," he continues before I can answer. "I'm from the suburbs of

Boston, but my grandparents had a place on the Jersey Shore for most of my childhood. I mean, I guess we're technically still in our childhoods, but you know what I mean."

I nod. "My grandparents mostly live in Florida," I tell him. "But, like, dull Florida."

"Not near the beach and not near Disney World?" he asks.

"Exactly," I say, and I feel a grin spread across my face despite myself. I quickly pull my lips over my teeth, hiding my braces, and I try to change the subject. "So have you been to New York before?"

"I have," Tate answers as my phone begins to vibrate incessantly. I look down and see Celia's face on my screen, calling me again.

"Sorry," I tell him, silencing Celia's call. "So you have been here before?"

"Yeah, my family comes down quite a bit," he answers. "How about you?"

"Only twice," I tell him as, yet again, my phone begins going to town. I hit decline and shove the phone deep into my pocket.

"Is everything okay?" Tate asks.

"Yeah, sorry, just my best friend," I explain. "I told her I couldn't talk now, but she's insistent." I see Sofia and Kensington enter the room as Roberto asks us to return to our seats so he can give us our photo quest for the day.

"See you later, @AvalonByTheC," Tate says as I follow my roommates down our row.

"Bye, @Tater . . . ," I begin. "You know, I can't take you seriously with that PhotoReady name."

"It's pretty great, right? Who doesn't like tater tots?"

I find myself smiling as we plop down into our seats, and Sofia says, much more loudly than I would like, "He is cute with a capital Q."

"Shhhh," I shush her. "Seriously, do you have to be so loud?"

"See, he *is* cute," Sofia persists at the same volume as before. "You wouldn't be getting so huffy about it if you didn't think so."

"It's not that," I begin, but thankfully, Roberto saves me with three booming claps to get our attention.

"So today," he starts, "we're going to be focusing on contrasts—old versus new, nature versus man-made, dark versus light, et cetera. You and your groups have the entire rest of the day to head out anywhere you like within city limits, and concentrate on all the contrasting elements you see. Specifically, of course, those you can capture in a photograph. All pictures you post today should be labeled #PhotoRetreatContrast, and tomorrow morning, we'll gather again to discuss your work. Any questions?"

A few people raise their hands as Sofia leans across and asks Kensington and me, "We're going together again, right?"

"Definitely," I agree.

"You only keep me around for my navigational prowess," Kensington says.

"Definitely," I say again, which causes Kensington to shove my elbow off the armrest.

"You'll all meet back here by five p.m. tonight for a group dinner, but lunch will be your choice." Roberto is speaking again. "Once you have your group—two to five people would be best—head into the hallway, and we'll assign a counselor to chaperone you."

"Hurry, let's try to manipulate the line to make sure we don't end up with Perfecto," Sofia says, and we all gather our bags and head for the door. As we maneuver our way out of the room, I look down and see a new text from Celia: *See? You forgot about me. Again.*

CHAPTER 16

Today, we don't question Kensington when she tells us—just tells us, without asking—that we're going to the High Line. Her work as a tour guide yesterday has convinced us that we should trust her, whether or not we've ever heard of the place she's taking us.

"Wait, is the High Line the old train tracks which they converted into a park?" I ask as we walk across the city, Sofia and I once again practically skipping to keep up with her.

"Yes," Kensington calls as she darts across Seventh Avenue, Sofia and me running in order to not be hit by a taxi. "It's a tad cliché at this point, but it will do."

"Why cliché?" Sofia asks.

"It's on the touristy side," Kensington explains. "Not too bad—at least not yet—but it's definitely become an attraction. The fact that New Jersey over here has heard of it speaks volumes."

"Thanks a lot," I say. "Can you slow down? We do have all day, you know."

"I'm not one to mosey," Kensington says, but she slows her pace anyway. I stop to take a photo, bending down on the sidewalk where I've spotted a single dandelion growing between the bricks.

"See, it's life growing, no matter what the odds," I say.

"That's because it's a weed," Kensington retorts. "Weeds are like the most irritating people in your life— they pop up when you least want to see them."

"You should put that on a cocktail napkin," Sofia says, and then she laughs at her own joke. Once I'm satisfied with the shot, I stand and gesture for Kensington to continue.

"I'm going to load this while we walk, so don't let me trip," I say.

"Wow, you're loading a picture already?" Sofia asks. "Trying to please Roberto?"

"More like trying to please @TaterTotter," Kensington

pipes up. "Now that she knows he's stalking her page, she wants to give Mister Emerald Eyes something to star."

"Will you stop it with that?" I ask. "I just like the picture."

"Sure you do," Sofia says. "He's cute. Admit it."

"Kensington is the one who's calling him Mister Emerald Eyes," I point out. "Why don't you ask her what *she* thinks about him?"

"Because I'm not the one who turned sunburn pink the second he opened his mouth to speak to me," Kensington says. "Plus, with that green scarf constantly wrapped around his neck, you'd have to be blind to not notice that his eyes match it almost exactly."

"Where are we, anyway?" I ignore her commentary, desperate to change the subject.

"West Village," Kensington answers, thankfully dropping the Tate teasing. "It's like the most confusing neighborhood in all of Manhattan, so unless you want to wind up in the New York Lost and Found, I suggest you keep up."

Sofia and I fall in line obediently as Kensington weaves—truly weaves, since the streets jut off in all directions—her way toward what I can only assume is the High Line. We pass blocks upon blocks of some of the most gorgeous houses I've ever seen—red and brown and tan brownstones with wide stoops, trees lining the curbs, and ivy crawling up many of their façades. I snap as many photos as I can, whether or not I think they show contrast, all without breaking stride too much on Kensington's speed.

"Oh, you know what? Wait a minute," Kensington says. "We should backtrack." She turns around and we slump along after her.

"It will be amazing if I still have feet by the time this week is over," Sofia says.

"Yes, I should have listened to my mom when she recommended I bring more comfortable shoes," I say. Mom—I almost forgot to check in with my family today. I'm surprised my phone isn't blowing up with a flurry of proof-of-life requests. I choose one of the best brownstone pictures I've taken and text it to my parents and Arden, captioning it, *Current status*, before coming one step away from plowing into Kensington as she grinds to a sudden halt.

"You've seen the smallest park in the city—now feast your eyes on the narrowest house," she says, pointing to the brick building in front of us. "Actually, it's probably better from across the street." She darts between two parked cars and only hastily looks both ways before continuing to the opposite sidewalk. Sofia and I follow her much more carefully before turning to examine the building.

"That's insane," Sofia says. "How wide is it?"

"Do I look like a guidebook?" Kensington asks. "I only know its location—and that it doesn't even have a full address. It's, like, seventy-five and a half, or something." Sofia and I both take a bunch of photos, each trying to beat the other to the punch of loading one on PhotoReady first. I make sure to capture the full width of the brownstone next to the house, which is more than double its size, so that the picture shows some degree of contrast. Then I label the photo *Small packages, continued*, and give it the correct #PhotoRetreatContrast label.

"Done!" I announce triumphantly.

"Arghhh, no!" Sofia calls out, stomping her foot. "Now if I post it, I'll look like a poseur."

"That's the price you pay for being a slowpoke!" I tell her, placing my arm around her slight shoulders and turning to Kensington. "Now, where to, oh captain?"

After some more West Village wandering (probably too much for Kensington's tastes), we eventually reach the southernmost entrance to the High Line. We climb a flight of stairs to the top of the platform, and immediately, I can tell why Kensington brought us here, touristy or not. At first glance, the place is little more than an aboveground park, but the closer you look, the more you notice the small details of what it once was, specifically the outlines from the old railroad tracks. The High Line is more like an art exhibit, with benches rising directly from its pavement and sculptures and murals sprinkled along its route. On our right, the city spreads out before us, but on our left, only a few blocks over, sits the Hudson River, and right across that, New Jersey. I'm happy to see it again, but I'm even more excited to see what the High Line has to offer, especially in terms of photos.

As we walk along, contrasts pop out at me everywhere I look: the greenery against the train tracks, the spherical sculpture next to the rectangular steps, the lounging sunbather lying in front of the harried businessman. I capture as many of them as I can, pointing my camera all around

me and sporadically dropping down to my knees, or rais-
ing the lens above my head, in order to find the right angle.
Kensington, Sofia, and I spread out to explore in our own
ways, and within moments, I am lost in concentration. So
lost that when a figure approaches and asks me what time
it is, it's all I can do not to jump five feet in the air. I whirl
around, only to find myself face-to-face with none other
than @TaterTotter himself.

"What—are—oh—you need the time?" I stammer,
sounding like a surefire idiot.

Tate laughs, but there's something kind about it. And
outside, in the bright light of midday, I can't help noticing that Sofia is right: Tate *is* cute.

"Just wanted to surprise you," he says.

"Did you, um, did you follow us here?" I ask. Maybe
this guy really *was* a stalker. And, cute or not, I'm not
sure having a strange boy secretly following us around
the city would be something that would make my parents comfortable.

Or make *me* comfortable, for that matter.

"You think I'd be that creepy?" he asks. "I promise
this is nothing but a pleasant coincidence."

"Where's your group?" I ask, looking around for

Sofia and Kensington. Where, exactly, was *my* group?

"Don't have one," he says. "I sort of pretended to be with two different groups, so the counselors could assume I went with the other one, and then I could sneak off on my own." He shrugs. "My roommates are obnoxious. It's like they both think they're the next Ansel Adams or something." I must look at him quizzically, because he follows up with, "Sorry, I guess that sounds obnoxious too. He's some old photographer, though honestly, that's the only fact I know. I've never seen one of his pictures."

"Thanks, but I was more surprised that you ignored Roberto's warnings," I tell him. "You're not afraid you'll get caught?"

"Nah, that's what makes it exciting," Tate says, a devious grin spreading across his face.

"You better watch out before Lulu—she was the counselor assigned to us today—sees you," I warn him.

"I'm pretty good at blending in with the crowd," he says, pushing his sunglasses up on top of his head, revealing his eyes, which are as Emerald City green as Kensington had hinted. His hair, which looked light brown in the dimness of the fake classroom, has the faintest streaks of blond sprinkled through it, the kind of natural highlights no hairstylist could replicate. And then, of course, there's that smile.

Kensington appears over my shoulder, snapping me back to the present. "Well, well, well, look what the wind blew in," she says. "Did you follow us here?"

"Boy, you two really don't think much of me, do you?" Tate answers. "@AvalonByTheC asked the same thing."

"Smart girl," Kensington says. "And you didn't answer my question."

"He came on his own," I explain. "Or so he says."

"Thanks a lot," Tate responds as Sofia joins us.

"What are you doing here?" she asks him immediately. "And where's your group?"

"Would you care to explain?" Tate asks me.

"He pretended to be with two different groups when we were leaving the classroom," I say. "So that both groups figured that he headed out with the other one, but really, he escaped."

"Impressive work," Kensington tells him. "I wouldn't expect such creative thinking from the likes of Boston."

"You really know how to hurt a guy," Tate answers her, feigning being stabbed in the heart. "I was about to go grab some lunch, if you guys want to join me."

"There's food up here too?" I ask.

"Not exactly, but it's attached to Chelsea Market," Tate says, pointing. "You can get anything you could imagine in there—I previewed it on my way over."

"I'm obviously in," Sofia says. "I'm starving, and plus, it will be nice to have someone besides Kensington bossing us around for once."

"Rude," Kensington says. "Go ahead, Boston. Show us what you've got." Tate heads down a long stretch of the High Line, and within a few steps, Kensington has overtaken him.

"I can't possibly walk that slow," she says. "I'll meet you guys in there." Sofia and I stroll on either side of Tate, down a flight of stairs and into a building that looks more like a factory than a place to grab lunch.

"It used to be the old Nabisco factory," Tate explains, as if reading my mind. The building is shaped like a tunnel, with small specialty stores dotting each side. We pass a bakery known for cupcakes, then a bakery known for brownies, then a bakery known for bread. A fish shop and a milk shop and a sandwich shop, and then a whole room filled with vendors selling olive oil or cheese or doughnuts or tacos.

"I'm never going to be able to decide," I tell them. "And did we lose Kensington?"

"Here I am," Kensington appears from behind a shaved-ice stand. "I haven't been to this place in a while—it's gotten a lot more overwhelming."

"Yes, way too many options," Sofia agrees. "I want to try everything."

"Here's an idea," Tate says. "We each go and pick two things that we'd like to eat—but we buy enough for all four of us. Then we meet again and have a smorgasbord."

"I like the way you think," Sofia says. "Should we have a time limit?"

"Twenty minutes," Tate answers. "Then meet outside the back door of the market, and we'll head onto the High Line to find a table."

"Deal," I say. The four of us scatter in opposite directions, and I try to concentrate on choosing the best two items for our potluck. But despite the never-ending sights and the wafts of salt and sugar and spice that assault my senses from every angle, another image keeps overtaking all of them in my mind: Tate.

CHAPTER 17

By the time we finish our mishmash of a lunch, I am so full that I'm certain I'm going to have to be physically rolled to our next destination. By some miracle, the four of us managed to choose a somehow balanced and completely delicious meal. After snapping some photos of our most "contrasting" concoctions (a red velvet cupcake next to a red beet salad, for instance), it was all we could do not to lick each and every takeout container clean.

"I so want to go lie down on that bench and take a nap," Sofia moans, sleepily resting her head against her palm.

"Agreed," I tell her. "I don't think I've ever been fuller in my life."

"Nope, up and at 'em," Tate says, rising to his feet. "You can't give in to the tiredness, or you'll never get out of it. What we need now is a walk. A Kenz-style walk."

"You mean walking a nontortoise pace?" Kensington asks, joining Tate. "I'm not even sure *I'm* up for the task, but I'll try." Sofia and I both struggle to stand as we clean up our accumulated trash. Tate and Kensington discuss where to go next—for someone who's not a native, he sure seems to know a lot about the city—and they lead us down the stairs and off the High Line, heading in the direction of the water.

"You haven't seen the Hudson River walk yet, right?" Tate asks Sofia and me, the four of us—even Kensington—meandering in a row down the sidewalk.

"Only from a distance," I tell him. "Kensington showed us last night."

"Oh, so you actually showed them something besides the Honey, I Shrunk New York City attractions?" he teases her. "Tiniest garden, tiniest house . . ."

Kensington smacks him on his arm as we merge past bicyclists to cross onto the path, only a metal fence separating us from the shores of the Hudson River. Tate points us right, and we begin our stroll, the midday sun bouncing off the water, trying its best to combat the harsh wind gusts. I cross my arms against my chest and try to rub the goose bumps off my arms, chilled despite the sunlight.

"You cold?" Tate asks.

"Not too much," I answer. "But it got awfully windy all of a sudden, right?"

"You look cold," Sofia says. "Which is ridiculous, since I'm the one used to a desert climate. *I* should be shivering right now."

"You're such a martyr," Kensington tells her sarcastically. "And it's always extra windy by the river. New York's version of a sea breeze."

"Here, take this," Tate says, beginning to uncoil the green scarf from around his neck. "You look like you're about to turn into a popsicle." He hands the scarf to me.

"Oh no, it's not that bad, really," I protest.

"I insist," Tate says, tossing the scarf around the back of my neck before jamming his hands in his pockets, now looking cold himself.

"I'm surprised that came off so easily," Kensington says. "The way you always have it wrapped around you, I assumed it must be holding your head on straight." Tate wobbles his head back and forth dramatically, as if testing Kensington's theory.

I arrange the scarf around my shoulders like a shawl, grateful for the burst of warmth. "Thank you," I tell him. "You promise to take it back when you get cold?"

Tate holds up his palm as if taking an oath. "Scout's honor," he promises.

"So do we have a destination in mind, or are we just wandering?" Sofia asks.

"Are you up for a long haul?" Tate replies. "Because if so, I have an idea."

"What's 'long'?" Sofia asks. "I have short legs."

"Forty blocks, give or take," Tate answers. "Peanuts, really."

"What's forty blocks from here?" I ask.

"Only the smallest subway door in all of New York City," Tate answers grandly. "Bet you didn't know about that one, did you, Kenz?"

"Where? The Columbus Circle stop?" she asks.

"Yes. There's a door there built for a wizard. A very short wizard."

"Let's do it," Sofia says. "We might as well keep up our Shrinking New York City tradition."

"I bet our chaperones talk about us," I say. "We have to be the group that goes to the weirdest places."

"Hey, speaking of . . . ," Sofia begins, glancing over her shoulder. "Where *is* Lulu?"

Kensington also turns. "I never paid attention to what she looks like."

"Do you think we should text her?" Sofia asks.

"She never gave us her number," I point out. "And she never took ours, either."

"I have it," Tate says. "She was our chaperone last night. And I already texted her while we were buying lunch. I told her we had teamed up with another group, with a different counselor, and that she was off the hook with us."

"But . . . ," Sofia begins. "That's not true. We didn't join another group."

Tate shrugs, that infectious grin spreading across his face. "What they don't know won't hurt them, right?"

I look back and forth from Sofia to Kensington, hoping one of them will speak up, will say this is a bad idea, will insist that we track down a counselor immediately. But neither of them looks overly concerned by Tate's news.

"What's up, @AvalonByTheC?" Tate asks, almost in a whisper as Kensington and Sofia pull ahead of us. "You okay?"

I think about telling Tate the truth, that I'm not comfortable lying like this. That I'm afraid we're going to get caught. But despite every instinct that warns me to put an end to this, to convince Sofia and Kensington that we need to get back in touch with a chaperone, that we can't risk getting kicked out of the retreat, I find myself responding, "Yeah, I'm great."

And Tate—he smiles. And just like that, I actually am. Great, that is.

And I stay great for the majority of the next three hours, pushing my worries out of my mind as the four of us have more fun than I've had in a long time. Tate even convinces Kensington (after we find New York City's smallest subway door, of course) to go for a stroll down Fifth Avenue—including a stop at the flagship Tiffany & Co.—an activity I know that she normally would have refused on account of being "touristy." But all three of us seem to listen to Tate, and trust Tate, and agree that Tate has made what was already our good time even better.

Until, that is, we arrive at the designated meeting spot for our group dinner. And we are late. Ten minutes late. Without a chaperone. Officially, undoubtedly caught.

And let's just say that Roberto is not happy.

Rather than immediately reaming us out, Roberto relegates us to a table in the corner of the restaurant, making clear that the consequences will be doled out after dinner. We sit tensely as we wait, looking back and forth among one another, trying to figure out what's going to happen next.

"They're going to send us home, aren't they?" Sofia asks in a forced whisper.

"They might," Kensington agrees, and even her usually stoic face has been replaced by a look of concern.

"Maybe we should apologize," I suggest. "Maybe if we explain what happened—"

"That we purposely 'lost' our chaperone? I don't think so," Kensington interrupts me as Tate passes us each a menu.

"Is there something else we can do?" Sofia asks. "I really don't want to get kicked out. We just got here."

"Hey—no one's getting kicked out," Tate says. "If it

comes to that, I'll take the blame. You three don't have anything to worry about."

"No, you can't do that," I say, pulling his scarf more tightly around my shoulders, suddenly chilled. "You shouldn't take the fall for us. That's not fair." I look across the table at Sofia and Kensington, who nod, opening their mouths to speak, but Tate begins first.

"Look," he starts, "the way I see it, we don't have control over what they decide to do to us anyway, correct? So let's not waste any more time fretting over it. Plus, I'm starving."

"Me too," Sofia says quietly.

"There's the surprise of the century," Kensington quips. "Okay, you're right. Let's not talk about it anymore. We might as well enjoy our last supper, so to speak." The three of them all look down at their menus, so I follow suit, trying to push away my apprehension. The restaurant features a fusion of Chinese and Japanese dishes, and I swoop my eyes over the food options, searching for words I recognize.

"Do you think I can get a plate of egg rolls?" Sofia pipes up. "That's what I want."

"Not if you expect me to be seen eating with you,"

Kensington says. "This place is famous for sushi—not for egg rolls."

"Ew, I don't eat anything raw," Sofia says. "It's not like fish thrive in Arizona. Landlocked state and all."

"I've never had sushi either, and New Jersey isn't landlocked," I reassure Sofia, but this comment only riles up Kensington more.

"Well, you're not in Arizona or New Jersey anymore, are you?" she says, and before we can stop her, she places the order for our entire table—all sushi, without a single egg roll to be found.

"When I wake you up in the middle of the night crunching through our snacks because I'm starving to death, you'll be sorry," Sofia tells her.

"You will eat it and you will like it," Kensington insists. But when our plates of sushi arrive, Sofia and I stare at it skeptically, trying to decide where to start (if at all).

"What's up, @AvalonByTheC?" Tate asks, picking up a piece of rice-enclosed fish.

"I have no idea what to do with this," I tell him honestly.

"Nothing to it," he says, and then in a faux television

announcer voice, he continues, "What we have here is a basic tuna roll. How do you feel about salt?"

"Love salt," I answer, and he dumps at least two tablespoons of soy sauce onto one piece.

"And spice?" he asks.

"Not as much."

"Only a little wasabi, then," he says, moving a small bit of green goo off the corner of my plate and placing it on the roll. "Now pretend this is tuna fish, but in its natural state. And feel free to eat with your hands. No need for chopsticks." I grip the piece between my thumb and index finger, take a deep breath, and make a move to bite it.

"No, no, all at once. Don't be polite," Tate corrects me, and dutifully, I place the entire roll on my tongue. I begin chewing, praying that I don't gag and spit the entire creation onto his lap. But to my surprise, the sushi is . . . delicious. Not as good as the Levain cookie, not even as good as the smorgasbord we put together at Chelsea Market, but still good. Once I've swallowed, I pick up the soy sauce and begin to drown another piece.

"What'd you think?" Tate asks.

"It was great," I tell him. "Though I kind of only tasted soy sauce. Not that I mean that as a bad thing."

"Soy sauce makes everything better," Tate agrees. I nod, watching Kensington attempt to force-feed a roll with an orange center to Sofia.

"I don't eat salmon!" Sofia is insisting.

"Please, I saw you pick up a cupcake crumb you had dropped on the ground at the High Line and put it in your mouth. You're not that picky. Pull yourself together," Kensington says, shoving the whole thing in her mouth despite Sofia's protestations.

"I'm glad I got you as my sushi instructor," I tell Tate.

"Do you think this seating arrangement happened by accident, @AvalonByTheC?" Tate asks, flashing his signature smile. I feel my face flush, and I make a point of pretending to concentrate fully on spreading a dot of wasabi onto my next roll. Before I can taste it, Roberto claps his hands three times directly behind us, causing my stomach to turn a somersault.

"Once you have finished your meal, you will all be heading back to your dorm rooms for the night. Let this serve as your warning—if anything like what went on today happens again, it will mean an automatic dismissal from the program. And to make sure no further funny business goes on"—while my back is to him, I can feel his eyes, plus the eyes of the entire rest of the retreat, staring at us—"your counselors have been instructed to duct-tape you into your rooms. If any of you try to break out during the night, we will be aware, and we will find you, and that will be the end of your retreat experience. Our intention had been to give you some leeway this week, but those privileges have since been revoked due to the actions of your fellow retreaters." Roberto stops talking, and low murmurs spring up across the restaurant, presumably all about us.

"Phew, at least we get to stay, right?" Sofia whispers. "But are they seriously going to duct-tape us into our rooms? Is that even allowed?"

"It was probably a clause on that safety form our parents signed," Kensington reasons. "The one where they essentially signed our lives away."

"Boy, this brings a new meaning to Dingymist Dorm, huh?" Sofia says, but I can't manage to smile at her. The rest of our sushi sits uneaten as the whole group is escorted away, counselors surrounding us on all sides like a bunch of prisoners. As we walk back, I sense what feels like a thousand eyes boring into the backs of our heads. We are now the "bad kids" who have ruined it for the rest of the class. I try to tell myself that this isn't my fault, but I know that I'm partly responsible. And by the time Sofia, Kensington, and I are locked—truly locked—in Room 609 that evening, I feel close to tears. Roberto is going to call our parents, right? And even if he doesn't, I'm most likely going to wind up telling them on my own, if only to try to relieve the feelings of guilt that are hovering in the middle of my chest.

With nowhere to escape within our cramped quarters, I climb onto my bunk and burrow deep under my blanket, head included. I open my texts, taking a deep breath and trying to decide how best to broach this with my family before Roberto can reach them first. It would probably be better to call, but then Sofia and Kensington would hear the conversation, and plus, I'm afraid I would cry.

I drum my fingers against the back of my phone, thinking. Maybe I'll tell Arden. Maybe I'll explain the whole thing to her, and have her relay the story to our parents. Arden could make it funny. Arden could lighten up the whole circumstance. Arden might even make me feel better in the process.

I begin typing a note to her, backspacing multiple times as I decide where to start. In the middle of this drafting, my phone buzzes with a new text.

Way to keep your promise.

CHAPTER 18

Oh, no. Celia. *In all that had happened today,* I had completely forgotten to call her, to text her, to think about her much at all. And she was right—I *had* promised. Even though she had told me to go to New York without her, even though she had said it was okay, I knew she was jealous. *Of course* she was jealous. *I* would be jealous, if I were in her position. As her best friend, I should have considered that when she made me swear to keep her updated, it wasn't only because she wanted to live vicariously through my experience. It was because she felt left out. And forgotten.

I was a bad friend. I used to be a good one, but I hadn't been this week.

Just like how I used to be a person who didn't get in trouble. Who didn't aimlessly follow a boy around a strange city. Who wasn't the reason an entire dorm full of people were currently duct-taped in their rooms.

Agreeing to come to this retreat was quite possibly the worst decision I ever made. It was turning me into a person I barely recognized anymore.

I'm sorry, I type to Celia. *I had a terrible day. I'm so sorry. I miss you.*

But hours later, by the time I finally manage to fall asleep, she still hasn't responded.

Our dorm room remains quieter than usual the next morning as the three of us move about, trying not to get in each other's way. Eventually, Ella pulls the duct tape off our door and releases us, like caged animals, into the hallway. As we make our way toward the elevators, it becomes obvious that we were the final room to be "freed"—one last punishment for the ringleaders of trouble.

"We really are the black sheep now, huh?" Sofia asks as we wait for the elevator, even perfecto Ella leaving us behind.

"Looks like they even let Tate out before us," Kensington observes. "That's low."

"Maybe they didn't want to punish his two roommates," I reason. "All three of us were troublemakers in our room—but only he was in his."

"We're such rebel youth," Kensington says as we step onto the elevator, making our way to breakfast. I carry Tate's green scarf in my hand—in the uncomfortable chaos of our return last night, I had forgotten to return it to him. Once in the cafeteria, I deposit it on an empty chair before joining Sofia and Kensington at the end of the buffet line, all while feeling like everyone in the room is watching us and whispering about us. The girls who ruined their nights.

"Where's Tate?" Sofia asks quietly. She piles her plate extra high today, seemingly making up for the uneaten sushi dinner last night. "I don't see him anywhere."

"I'm trying not to look around," I say. "I feel like everyone hates us."

"Who needs them?" Kensington says. "We had a great time yesterday, and that's all that matters, right?"

Sofia and I don't answer at first, and I get the feeling that she's about as used to getting in trouble as I am. But then she pipes up with, "You know what? You're right. I honestly don't care if the rest of these people like me. And to tell you the truth, I always care if people like me. It's kind of my thing. So this is a big deal."

I smile at this, though I can't get on board with their attitudes. It's not that I'm so desperate for everyone to like me—I'm pretty sure my avoidance behavior at our first meeting in the lobby made that clear—but I also *hate* when people I care about are upset with me. People like Celia. The fellow retreaters being mad, well, Kensington is right—it doesn't really matter much. But their disdain toward us also doesn't make me feel better.

"But seriously, where *is* Tate?" Sofia asks again once we sit down. "He's definitely not in here."

"Maybe they didn't release him yet?" Kensington guesses. "Freed his roommates but not him?"

"Do you think I should give this to one of the counselors?" I ask, holding up his scarf. "Ask one of them to return it to his room?"

"I'm surprised he let that thing out of his sight for this long," Kensington says. "He had it on since the minute I met him, until, of course, he gave it to you." She bats her eyelashes quickly, mocking me, which makes Sofia laugh.

"He definitely likes you," Sofia adds. "For him to give up his security blanket for you? That means a lot."

I roll my eyes, tossing the scarf on the table as if it were burning my hand. At the time, I was happy when Tate had lent it to me, both because I *was* cold, and because, well, it was nice. Tate was nice.

But now, the sooner I can get that thing out of my possession, the better. Thinking back, my day was going great before I put on the scarf. Its presence was the beginning of my bad luck: getting in trouble with Roberto, hurting Celia's feelings, wishing to flee home. . . .

That scarf, I believe, is cursed.

"I'm going to ask," Kensington interrupts my thoughts, making a beeline toward Ella, Nina, and Lulu, who are huddled together on the other side of the room. Kensington's back is toward us, so we can't watch her face, and when she turns around to walk back, she remains difficult to read. She takes her seat and pulls off a corner of her croissant without speaking.

"Well?" I ask, unable to take the suspense any longer.

"He got kicked out," Kensington answers.

"No way!" Sofia yells as I feel my own mouth drop open. "Are you lying?"

"Nope," Kensington says. "It's true."

"Because of yesterday?" I ask. "But that's not fair—we can't let him take the blame for us, even if he said he would. We were just as responsible as he was, and if he got kicked out for being late and not being with a chaperone, then we should—"

"Not about yesterday," Kensington interrupts me. "It seems Mister TaterTotter managed to open his duct-taped door last night and sneak out. There was some kind of pattern to how the counselors had taped them closed, and they could tell it had been tampered with." Kensington shrugs. "At that point, he was kind of asking for it, right?"

"I can't believe it," Sofia says. "I mean, I believe he did that—it sounds just like Tate—but still. He didn't even say good-bye."

"I doubt they gave him a chance to go around and tell people to keep in touch," Kensington says. "I wouldn't be surprised if Roberto refused to let him pack."

"Wait, then what am I supposed to do with *that*?" I say, pointing to the scarf, which is lying limply in the middle of the table. "How do I get it back to him?"

"Keep it," Kensington says, a wry smile parting her lips. "Something to remember him by." This comment makes Sofia cackle, and they lean their foreheads together, laughing.

Laughing *at* me.

"Never mind," I say testily, rising and grabbing the offensive scarf, ready to give it to the counselors—or anyone but me—to deal with. I have to get it out of my sight, and out of my life, before it causes any additional damage.

"Wait, no," Sofia calls after me. "If you give it to the counselors, they'll probably lose it on purpose, as some sort of revenge on Tate." She begins scrolling through her phone. "Did he give either of you his number?"

"No, none of us ever exchanged them," I say, standing behind them with my hands on my hips, the scarf dragging on the floor next to me.

"That was dumb. We should have," Sofia says. "I'll try to send him a message through PhotoReady, or comment on one of his pictures or something."

"He has that feature turned off," I tell her. "He mentioned that. Something about not wanting to give anyone the expectation that he'd respond." I look down at the scarf, as if staring at it long enough would make it disappear. I should leave it here, unclaimed, and hope that its removal from my life would also mean the removal of all the bad energy circling around me. Then, like Tate did, maybe I could find a way to vanish, to run home, to get away. Maybe I could go to Celia's house, to apologize in person. Maybe Arden could convince our parents to come home early, and they could pick me up. Maybe by tonight, I could be asleep in my own room, on my own sheets, under my own covers. And then maybe I could turn back into the person I was a few days ago. The one who had never met Sofia, or Kensington, or Tate. The non-worldly, non–boy following, nontroublemaking Avalon. The one who was content with what was outside her windows.

I spend most of our class time plotting how to get home. I've already texted Arden, who was no help whatsoever (it seems she and my grandmother are on the verge of winning first place in this week's pinochle tournament, and she isn't about to give that up). Plus, I didn't want to tell her the real reason I wished to leave, at least not yet.

There was no indication that Roberto had told our parents what had happened, so I didn't want to sound that alarm bell unless necessary.

Not one of my, nor Kensington's nor Sofia's, photos is chosen by Roberto to be featured in class today, though whether that's because we took lousy shots or because he is purposely discriminating against us is anyone's guess. From the little I listen at the end of class, our mission today is to go on a shadow trek—to use the day's sunlight to play with what is lit, and what is camouflaged. With no solid leads on a way home, I reluctantly follow my roommates to the subway (with Nina very close behind us—it seems the counselors aren't going to risk another disappearing act by Room 609). Kensington has decided to lead us to the streets of SoHo—with their relatively short buildings and narrower streets, she thinks the shadows cast will be more interesting than those farther uptown (at least, this is the reasoning she gives us, not that Sofia or I are in a position to argue with her navigational know-how at this point).

I keep glancing at my phone on the subway, ignoring Sofia and Kensington's chatter and hoping for an *I forgive you* text to appear from Celia. When we reach our stop and walk up to street level, I decide to bite the bullet and call her. I can't take the silent treatment for a second longer, and if I can't apologize in person, this will have to do.

"Guys, I need to make a phone call real quick," I yell after them, but Kensington and Sofia are already galloping ahead. I scramble to catch up while dialing Celia, and I watch them collapse into giggles—true, laugh-out-loud giggles—as I wait for my phone to ring. I hold my free ear closed with my finger, remaining a few yards away from them so I can hear. But five rings later, when the phone clicks over to Celia's voice mail, I hang up. Celia and I have agreed to never leave each other voice mails, because we both think they're annoying. So now is definitely not the time to make her even more upset by breaking one of our main friendship rules.

That is, if I didn't already break the *Don't be a lousy, selfish friend* rule beyond repair.

"What are you guys laughing at?" I walk up to Sofia and Kensington, who are huddled in the same place, Kensington propped against the railing of a stoop and Sofia leaning on a tree, sputtering with laughter.

"She stepped in dog poop," Sofia tells me, pointing wildly at Kensington.

"And then *she* stepped in the same poop," Kensington fills in, tears in the corners of her eyes from laughing. A couple of days ago, I never would have believed that Kensington would be capable of such laughter, period. And it would have been a welcome surprise to see this side of her, if I weren't completely out of the loop on the story behind it.

"Come on, let's take a selfie," Sofia says. "We have to document this moment." She holds up her phone and the three of us crowd our heads into the frame. Sofia clicks the button and when the photo appears, the image causes them to burst out laughing all over again.

"How did we *both* close our eyes?" Kensington asks. "Now this is getting weird." My eyes are open in the photo, but it doesn't even matter. Because not only am I not in on the joke, I'm also barely in the picture. My head is there, but while Kensington's and Sofia's faces are in full lighted view, I am, quite literally, standing in their shadows. Dim and hardly there at all.

And at this moment, that's exactly how I feel.

CHAPTER 19

I try—I really do—to enjoy the beginnings of our tour of SoHo. I attempt to make the best of it, to push my now overwhelming desire to go home out of my mind. But as the three of us, Nina close on our heels, hustle through the window-shoppers, dodging strollers and dog leashes and more than a few tourists, I can't manage to get excited, to look for great shadow pictures, or to engage with Sofia and Kensington, who seem to be getting closer and chummier by the minute. I wonder what would happen if I feigned illness, if I pretended I was suddenly and violently sick. Would Nina escort me back to our dorm room, where I could at least be by myself for a few hours? Even better, would they call my parents? Would I get to go home?

"What is *with* you, Avalon Kelly?" Kensington's voice snaps me back to the present. "You are Mopey McCrankerson today."

"Sorry," I say. "I'm not feeling so hot."

"You mean you're not feeling so *hot*," Kensington says, fanning herself with her hand. "Because your little crush isn't around anymore." I feel my face grow warmer no matter how hard I try to stop the blushing.

"Ooh, you're right," Sofia says. "The pink cheeks are giving you away, Av." I roll my eyes and attempt to step around them, but they block my path.

"And to think—you were so close to becoming the next Mrs. Avalon TaterTotter," Kensington continues, which causes she and Sofia to squeal with laughter.

"Guys, just stop, okay? You're *not* funny." The words feel like they come out of nowhere, like someone other than me said them. Sofia and Kensington stare at me, stunned, as if a stranger has replaced their roommate.

"Whoa," Kensington says under her breath. And then, it happens. As much as I try to prevent it, as much as I had managed to hold them in before, they come: the tears. They start to drop, heavy and furious, down my cheeks, and the more frantically I struggle to force them away, the harder they fall.

"Hey, hey, hey." Sofia is next to me, arms around my shoulders, cradling me like Mom would do when I was little. "What's wrong? What happened? What can we do?"

"Yeah, all of that," Kensington says. "Look, I'm not much of a hugger, but what she said."

"Sorry," I say, wiping my wrist against my face. "Sorry. I don't know why I'm crying."

"Yes, you do," Kensington insists. "Tell us. We can't fix it unless you tell us."

"I don't know," I tell them honestly. "I'm kind of homesick today. And I'm not used to getting in trouble. And my best friend is mad at me."

"Celia?" Sofia asks, and I nod. "I know of her from Avalon's PhotoReady page," she explains to Kensington.

"That's because you're a creeper," she says. "Why is she mad at you?" she asks me.

I take a deep breath and rush through the story as quickly as possible. How Celia is the one who found out about the retreat, how she wanted us to come to it together. How we were both wait-listed, but then I got in and she didn't. How I had promised her that I would keep her updated while I was here—how I would make her feel like she was a part of the retreat too—but I was so busy running around the city with them (and having fun, to boot) that I had all but forgotten about her. And now, how Celia wasn't speaking to me, how her feelings were clearly hurt, how she was jealous, and how, because of all this, I feared our entire friendship was damaged for good.

For a second, once I finish, I fear Sofia and Kensington are going to take one look at each other and start laughing—uncontrollably giggling, like they did about the dog poop—all over again. I mean, hearing the story out loud, it sounds so ridiculous, so petty, so immature. And Sofia and Kensington, well, they're not immature. Kensington, especially. I'm sure she's never cried hysterically on a street corner because someone didn't text her back. Once I looked at the whole thing from a distance, it sounded so childish.

Which didn't mean I still wasn't upset by it.

"What was this chick's photo project?" Kensington breaks the silence. "The one that didn't get her into the retreat?"

"#CeliaHeartsNYC," I tell her. "Like the 'I Heart NY'

T-shirts, only she took photos of things that looked like hearts."

"So, easy," Kensington says. "Find her some hearts. There have to be tons around the city. Continue her corny project for her, which is probably what she would have done if she had been accepted on the retreat, right? That will show that you care more than some pathetic apology text would."

"I agree," Sofia says, releasing her arm from around my shoulders. "Well, not about the 'corny' and 'pathetic' parts." She shoves Kensington as she says this. "But about the meaning behind it. Plus, even if Celia is ignoring your calls and texts, she's probably checking Photo-Ready, so she'll be sure to see it."

I had to hand it to Kensington—for a girl who seemed so utterly unsentimental (she didn't bring a single personal item from home to our dorm room!), this was a pretty thoughtful idea.

But it was also an idea that I was almost positive Celia wouldn't like.

"Thank you," I say. "Really. That's such a nice idea. But . . ."

"What?" they ask at the same time.

"I don't think Celia will go for it," I explain. "She was pretty possessive about her project—like whenever I found a heart, I would send it to her so *she* could post it. I don't know. I feel like maybe she'll interpret it like first I stole her retreat, and now I'm stealing her project."

"I'd like to go on record as saying that I never want to meet this girl," Kensington states. "But fine, then do something else—come up with your own photo collection about her."

"Cs!" Sofia blurts out. "Instead of hearts, you can look for Cs!"

"Cs?" Kensington asks.

"For Celia," Sofia explains. "And plus—arghh, I can't believe I didn't think of this!" She claps her hands over her open mouth, her eyes wide with excitement. "@AvalonByTheC! Get it? The C! So it's like a double pun, or whatever."

"That's . . . ," I begin, and Kensington and Sofia both look at me like they think I'm about to shoot down this idea too. "That's . . . brilliant. It's absolutely, amazingly brilliant. I can't guarantee it will work, but *I* love it."

"What are you going to call it?" Sofia asks, literally

bouncing up and down on the pavement, beyond proud of herself.

I think for a moment and then answer, "How about #iCnyc? But with only the first C capitalized, so that it stands out."

"Perfecto," Kensington answers, which coming from her is funnier than it should be.

"Thank you," I tell them. "For understanding. I know it might sound dumb. But I—"

Kensington holds up her hand, halting me. "The way I see it, if this plan makes you stop blubbering with tears like a weepy jellyfish—"

"A weepy jellyfish?" Sofia interrupts her.

"Just go with it," Kensington says, but then it's my turn to stop them.

"There is one more thing," I say, digging in my bag and pulling out the green scarf. "What am I going to do with this?"

"I thought you had left it in the cafeteria," Kensington says.

"I couldn't go through with it," I say. "Like you said, Tate loves this scarf—I couldn't abandon it."

"I guess that means tying it to a random street lamp

is out of the question too," Sofia jokes, taking the scarf from me and wrapping it around her own head.

"Be careful with that—I think it might be cursed," I warn her. "Everything started going downhill after I put it on yesterday." Sofia removes it and tosses it dramatically in Kensington's direction. It lands on her shoulder, where she ignores it, swiping furiously at her phone instead.

"What are you looking at so intently?" I ask her.

"You really want to give the scarf back?" she asks. "I think I know how."

"How?" Sofia questions.

Kensington holds out her phone, and I recognize Tate's PhotoReady feed. He's posted more pictures since yesterday, but they're not the ones from our day together.

"Is that Boston?" Sofia asks, squinting at the photos. "Is he home already?"

Kensington stomps her foot with mock rage. "You've been here three days and you don't recognize the place? The pictures are from here. Tate is still in New York. And I bet we can find him."

CHAPTER 20

"No. No way," I shoot down Kensington's idea immediately, taking the scarf off her shoulder and tying it tightly around the strap of my bag. "I'll give the scarf to Roberto and have him mail it back. Or something."

"That's much less fun," Kensington says. "Plus, you're right—I'd bet money that the scarf would purposely get 'lost in the mail,' just for spite. If you want to return it, safe and sound, you're going to have to do so in person."

"No," I repeat. "Tate got us in enough trouble yesterday. We're not chasing after him."

"Who said anything about chasing?" Kensington asks. "Plus, wouldn't you like to see him again?"

"If he wanted to be seen, he would have given us a way to contact him," I point out.

"We should do it," Sofia says. "We should at least try. If only to return the scarf. The cursed scarf."

I smile despite myself. "I *would* like to get rid of this thing," I confess, looping one of its ends around my hand. "Without actually, you know, *getting rid* of it."

"Then it's on," Kensington announces. "Let's go. To the subway and out of SoHo. I've had about as many cobblestones as I can take for one day anyway."

"Where are we going?" Sofia calls after her.

"Bloomingdale's," Kensington replies. "Now pick up your hooves and follow me." She leads us to the correct subway station, Nina sticking close behind us.

"So he's at Bloomingdale's?" Sofia asks Kensington. "Or do you want to go shopping?"

"He's there. I recognized the background from the last picture he posted," Kensington says. "Which was eight minutes ago."

"This is exciting," Sofia says as we board the train. "I feel like we're on a stakeout."

"In stakeouts, don't you sit somewhere and lie in wait?" I ask. "This is more like a high-speed chase." As if on cue, our subway grinds to a harsh halt.

"High speed, in this case, is relative," Kensington says, a mumbling voice coming over the intercom.

"What's he saying?" I whisper.

"Something about a delay," she says. "Don't worry—happens all the time."

"We're never going to catch up to him at this rate," Sofia says with a sigh, slouching in her seat. "We'll be stuck with that cursed scarf forever."

"Please don't say that," I beg while flipping through the photos on my phone. "You want to help me while we wait?"

"It's not like we have anything else to do," Kensington says, leaning over my shoulder. "What's up?"

"I'm looking for letter *C*s from the pictures I took the past few days," I say. "I figure I'll get a head start, since who knows how many we'll find today?"

"The High Line," Kensington states instantly. "Didn't you go all the way to the top section, where the track curves around Hudson Yards? That would look like a *C*, if you managed to take a picture of it."

"It pains me to say this, but you might be a genius," I say, opening a photo of exactly what Kensington is describing. "Do you think Celia will get it if I start with this one?"

"Maybe not," Sofia says. "But it's a great photo anyway. Very New York."

"Good point," I say, quickly giving the picture a black-and-white filter and then posting it on Photo-Ready with the label #iCnyc. "Wait, I think I took a picture of the Levain cookie that might work. Let me see." I scroll through my photos again, and as predicted, there's one of my cookie, a few bites taken out of the side. If I rotate the picture around to the correct angle, it totally looks like a *C*. I show it to Kensington and Sofia.

"Great, now find one more before we get off," Kensington says as our train jolts to a start. "Rule of threes and all."

"Isn't it the rule of thirds?" Sofia asks. "And I don't think it means to post three—"

"Whatever, brainiac," Kensington interrupts her. "You get my point." I post the cookie picture, and then I find another photo I had taken of a bicycle pulled into a rack, with only half of its wheel showing. I hold it up for Kensington and Sofia to study, as if asking permission.

"I think it works," Sofia says. "And now, besides keeping our eyes peeled for Tate, we'll also have to look for Cs."

"Thanks," I say. "I hope she gets what I'm doing."

"She at least can't say you didn't try," Sofia says.

"And if she does, maybe it's time to get some new friends," Kensington quips, standing to exit the train as we reach the next stop. And though I don't say it out loud, I know that's a huge reason why Celia's hurt right now—the fact that I *have* made new friends. And as much as I don't want to lose my best one, I can't say that I regret having met the two I have beside me.

The good news is that right around Bloomingdale's, I find three more Cs: the sleek curve of a metal door handle, the left side of a round window at the top of a town house, and the C in the sign for Dylan's Candy Bar (Kensington said that last one was cheating, but I didn't care).

The bad news is that by the time we reached Bloomingdale's, Tate had already posted a new picture from a different location—one Kensington recognized as being from a completely different corner of Manhattan.

"I can't believe he went to South Street Seaport," she murmurs as we make our way back to the train. "I thought he had better taste than the tourist hubs."

"Do you think we should go all the way there, or should we wait for him to post his next picture?" I ask. "It seems like by the time we get there, he'll be gone anyway."

"Maybe he's not even posting them in order," Sofia guesses. "Maybe that picture was from earlier."

"No, it's not," Kensington says, pulling up the photo of South Street Seaport again. "See, if you look at the clock in the center of the square, it says the time. Which means the picture was taken only a couple of minutes before he posted it."

"Now it pains *me* to say this," Sofia tells her. "But perhaps you really are a genius."

"Guilty as charged," Kensington states. "Now move it or lose it. Or more aptly, lose *him*." We shuffle back down the stairs to the subway, and I open PhotoReady as we wait for the train to arrive. I've gotten a few stars on my #iCnyc pictures, but not one of them is from Celia.

"You know what they say about watched pots," Kensington says, and I look up to see her, arms crossed, watching me scroll through my notifications. "And there's another C. You should be paying attention to your surroundings." Kensington is pointing to a poster for the ballet, the dancer's leg curved around behind her so that her heel is almost touching the top of her head. Kensington is right—if looked at correctly, it forms a perfect C.

"This is why we keep you around," I tell her, snapping the photo as Kensington smirks. "So I hate to point this out, but have we taken a picture of a single shadow today?"

"Oh, right, I almost forgot about that," Sofia says, twirling around and searching for one.

"Please, I thought that was a dumb assignment anyway," Kensington says. "And plus, what's the worst Roberto can do to us at this point? Not show our pictures during class? Oops, he already does that. Duct-tape us in our rooms? That's covered too. Send us home? We leave Friday anyway—seems like it would be a waste of his resources at this point."

"Maybe we should make a big show of at least taking a couple," I suggest. "If only so Nina doesn't get too suspicious about why we're darting around town."

"Fine," Kensington sighs, looking toward the tracks.

"Ooh, look at that ray of light shining through the ceiling." She says this part loudly for Nina's benefit. "I bet it's creating a shadow." She turns and gives Sofia and me a mischievous look as she takes the photo, and I have to bite the insides of my mouth to keep from laughing.

And even though not much has changed since this morning—we're still the enemies of the PhotoRetreat, Tate's cursed scarf is still in my possession, and Celia is still not speaking to me—the day feels like it has shifted dramatically. Out of the shadows, and finally, back to the sunshine.

CHAPTER 21

As we had feared, at almost the exact second we reach the boats of South Street Seaport, Tate posts a new picture—this one in a location that even Kensington doesn't recognize. At this news, I bury the scarf in the deepest corner of my bag, resigned to push it out of my mind, curse and all. "Maybe Roberto will give me Tate's home address," I suggest. "That way, I can make sure the scarf gets returned. And we can stop this wild-goose chase."

"But this wild-goose chase is fun," Sofia protests. "And wouldn't you like a chance to say good-bye?"

"Why are you making this all about me?" I ask. "You two spent just as much time with Tate as I did."

"Yeah, but he liked you more," Sofia says.

"He didn't like—" I try to object, but Sofia cuts me off.

"Don't get antsy—I'm not saying you two are getting married or anything," she says. "But it was obvious that he made it a point to talk to you. So I think it would be nice if you—if we all—got to say good-bye."

"I'm begging you," I begin. "Can we not do this? There's so much of New York we haven't seen yet—let's forget about Tate." Kensington and Sofia glance at each other.

"Okay, fine," Kensington relents. "But what about the curse?" She twists her fingers into claw shapes and cackles like a witch, mocking us.

"Very funny," I say. "Let's hope it doesn't have an effect when the scarf is out of sight. Plus, we survived the whole morning without incident."

"Save for your little SoHo meltdown," Kensington says. "Not to mention the dog poop. But okay. Do you want to wander around here for a bit? It's full of tourists—right up your alley." And so, we spend the remainder of the afternoon frolicking around the Seaport before making the long trek back to our dorm by foot, this time being sure to get there in plenty of time for dinner. And that night, for the first time all week, I am so utterly exhausted from our day—and from the previous nights of restlessness—that I fall asleep as soon as my head hits the pillow. And I stay asleep until the morning sun is bursting through our window, making the glow of the twinkle lights all but irrelevant.

When I sit up on my bunk, crouching slightly so that my head doesn't hit the ceiling, I'm temporarily convinced that I must still be asleep. I rub the sides of my hands against my eyes as if to clear my vision, and then I stare again.

Across the room, above Kensington's sleeping form, Sofia's and my mural of pictures seems to have quadrupled overnight. Images of our week, ones I recognize from all three of our PhotoReady accounts, rise from every angle, colliding together to form a patchwork of our time together. I laugh out loud in delight before clapping my hands over my mouth, but it's too late. I hear Sofia turning in the bed beneath me, and Kensington flips onto her back.

"I take it you like it?" she asks in her groggy sleep voice.

"I don't even know what to say," I tell her, climbing down the ladder to the floor and shaking Sofia fully awake.

Sofia looks grumpy as she rises into a seated position, but the grimace on her face disappears the second she turns to Kensington's side of the room. "Arghhhhhh," she screams. "What did you do? That is crazy amazing!"

"Good thing you two sleep like the dead," Kensington says. "I thought for sure that your nineteenth-century printer was going to wake you as I worked, but you were both snoring away."

"Hey, I don't snore," I say. "But whatever—really, you outdid yourself." I crawl onto Kensington's bed so I can get a better look at the images. "Wait, I didn't post this one on PhotoReady. Or this one either."

"I stole your phones, duh," Kensington says. "There were some real gems in there, let me tell you."

"Oh, I almost forgot about this," Sofia says, pointing to the photo I had accidentally snapped of her bursting through the door of our room. "Too bad we didn't capture the same kind of picture of *your* arrival." She says this to Kensington.

"You mean when we hated one another?" Kensington asks. "Yes, that definitely should have been preserved in print."

We scan the rest of the pictures, laughing and

reminiscing over the shots. "Hey, where did you stash our phones?" Sofia asks.

"On the desk. I even charged them for you," Kensington says. "I'm a full-service operation."

"After you stole them, it's probably the least you could do," I say as Sofia fetches hers and then scrolls down her screen. "Did Celia star any of my photos yet?" I ask her.

"Will you stop worrying about her?" Kensington says. "While you're here, you still have us. And once you're home, she's going to have to get that bug out of her butt eventually." And while I realize Kensington is most likely right, it doesn't stop me from taking a picture out our dorm room window of the last traces of the moon in the far corner of the sky. It is, after all, in its crescent form, and shaped just like a *C*.

Once again, none of our shadow pictures were featured during the morning discussion—the price we pay, I suppose, for spending more time concentrating on finding *C*s. And on trying to locate the owner of a possibly unlucky green scarf.

"So should we see where Tate has headed today?" Kensington asks, pulling out her phone as we head outside.

"No," I stop her. "I think we should try to focus on the assignment. It's our last full day in New York together. We should spend it doing what we actually came here to do."

"Look at you getting all sentimental," Kensington says.

"Yes," I say with a grin. "But also, I left the scarf in our room—on purpose—so we wouldn't get distracted. So now, no reason to even consider it. Or its possible curse."

"Sneaky, sneaky," Sofia says. "So what *is* our assignment for today? I swear, Roberto's voice is like the teacher in *Charlie Brown* to me—whomp whomp whomp."

"Motion," I say. "Whatever that means. Isn't it hard to capture motion with only our phones? I feel like those pictures always turn out blurry."

"We don't necessarily have to be literal about it," Kensington says. "Now, any special requests for today?"

"I propose that we let Sofia choose at least one place," I suggest. "It's still her first time in New York, so if she wants us to tourist it up, let's go for it."

"Fine," Kensington drags out the word like it's a big sacrifice. "What'll it be, Arizona?"

"How about . . . ," Sofia begins.

"Please don't say Times Square, please don't say Times Square, please don't say Times Square," Kensington begins murmuring, loudly enough that I know we're supposed to hear.

"Central Park?" Sofia suggests.

"Perfect," Kensington says, and I look over my shoulder.

"I think you mean 'perfecto,'" I say, pointing to the counselor who has been assigned to us today: none other than Ella.

"Now it's more important than ever that we keep our distance," Kensington says seriously. "I don't mean, like, run away again or anything. But we do not engage her. Got it?"

"She hasn't been nearly as friendly since the whole duct tape incident anyway," I point out. "I bet she leaves us alone. So . . . Central Park?"

"Yeah, come on," Kensington says. "But I'm warning you that we're not starting at the castle or the zoo or the reservoir—nothing from the top-five section of a guidebook."

"So where are we headed?" I ask.

"Haven't you learned to trust my judgment by now?"

Kensington asks. So as usual, Sofia and I fall in step behind her, following her blindly into our day.

It turns out Kensington's plan is to take us to the north end of Central Park to a place called the Conservatory Garden, which lies behind a giant black gate off of Fifth Avenue. Unlike most other areas of the park, this section looks like a palace estate, so pristine in its layout that a castle would not seem out of place. Sofia, Kensington, and I skip around like little kids, snapping photos of the bubbling fountain (motion) or a flower with half its petals missing (C), or simply one another, enjoying our time. It is one of the most relaxing, and most fun, experiences I've had all week, and I make a point to take a moment to sit on one of the garden's benches to appreciate it. All at once, I am nostalgic for this retreat, even though it's not over yet. Not that I won't be okay with going home—pleased, even—but it turns out that those who convinced me to come to New York were right: This was an opportunity I couldn't pass up, one that may never come again. No matter what the problems from the past couple of days, I was truly happy I had come.

"Are you ready, Thoreau, or are you going to sit there

all day?" Kensington calls from across the garden, breaking my personal reverie. I hop up and begin to head toward her, but the arm rest of the bench catches my eye.

"Be right there!" I call, and I take a photo of the curved iron, which, when I tilt the camera just so, looks exactly like a *C.* I post the picture on PhotoReady as I walk to join my roommates. Celia still hadn't contacted me—or starred a single photo in the series—which bothered me, though I tried not to let it.

But then a new fear crosses my mind: Maybe Celia doesn't realize the series is for her. Maybe she thinks it's some kind of retreat inside joke, and it's making the problems between us worse. I should have told her about the *C*s right after I posted the first picture. I should have explained, even if I wasn't sure she was listening.

I open our silent text chain and write, *#iCnyc. C for Celia. C for @AvalonByTheC.* And then, I have a brilliant idea—something that I would call Kensington a genius over, if she had come up with it. I know precisely which item I need to use to finish my #iCnyc project.

I pull out my Room 609 key with the key chain from Celia attached: the key chain with the *A* and *C* in its design. Celia had said the two letters were based on my

PhotoReady name, but they also represented Avalon and Celia, A and C, together. Always.

I hadn't thought of the connection until now, but it was perfect. Maybe even meant to be.

Maybe even perfecto.

CHAPTER 22

It seems that the trip to the Conservatory Garden had put Kensington in a good mood, since she then allowed us to stroll (not even run-walk, but truly stroll) blocks upon blocks of Fifth Avenue. We walked past the Museum of the City of New York, past the Smithsonian Design Museum, and past the Guggenheim. We photographed the rushing taxis on the street, the rushing people on the sidewalks, and the rushing bicyclists on the sidewalk who were supposed to be on the street. We sauntered all the way to the Metropolitan Museum of Art, where, instead of passing by, Kensington led us up the grand steps to the front doors and brought us inside.

"We're having lunch," she said matter-of-factly. "We

have a family membership here, so I can get you two in for free." After we had been given our admittance stickers, Kensington had led us through the museum, past hundreds of classic pieces of art, all the way to a hidden back elevator, which dropped us off on the fourth floor. This is where the Met's Members Dining Room is—the place that you're only able to eat in if you're a member.

We had been seated against the window, a gorgeous view of Central Park right at our fingertips. And though Kensington had deigned to ask Ella if she wanted to join us, we can't say we were unhappy when she said she would walk around the museum and to text her when we were finished (she did cap off these instructions with "And no funny business this time," which I thought was unnecessary). Never before in my life had I felt more grown-up, more sophisticated, more like someone who *of course* has lunch at the Metropolitan Museum of Art's exclusive dining room.

And more like a New Yorker.

"Are we boring you, Short Stack?" Kensington asks Sofia as she obsessively scrolls through her phone, ignoring the scene around her.

"I'm so behind on my PhotoReady feed," Sofia complains. "The three of us took some amazing shots today, by the way. We should print them for our mural."

"For the one night we have left?" I ask.

"Why not?" Sofia says. "Hey, wait a minute." She pauses, staring steadily at her screen. "Have you heard from Celia yet?"

"No," I answer. "I texted her and explained the #iCnyc project, since I was afraid she didn't understand that it was for her. But still nothing."

"Well, it appears she finally got it," Sofia says, holding up her phone for Kensington and me to see. There on PhotoReady, I find a photo of a picture frame, one I recognize from Celia's room. Inside the frame is the very first picture Celia and I took together in elementary school after we had become friends. On the corner of the frame, Celia has pasted a bright red construction paper heart, and she has captioned the shot, *Thank you @AvalonByTheC for being the best #BigAppleBFF ever. Can't wait to C you so soon! #iCnyc #CeliaHeartsNYC*

"Happy now, Avalon Kelly?" Kensington asks. "It seems the squabble heard around the world is over."

"Hold on," I say, whipping out my own phone. "I need to be the first to star it."

"Oh, brother," Kensington says, dropping her head back dramatically and groaning toward the ceiling.

"Thank you both for helping me," I tell them as I post a quick comment on Celia's page. "I know it sounds silly to you, but it was important to me. So thank you."

"Anytime," Sofia says.

"Now can we please wrap up this enterprise so we can enjoy our lunch in peace?" Kensington asks. With that, Sofia and I deposit our phones in our bags, and we resume our conversation, falling into the comfortable chatter of three New Yorkers out on the town.

Once we finish our meal, Sofia obediently texts Ella to tell her that we're ready to leave, and we meet her on the front steps of the Met. Ella offers to take photos of us standing on the steps together—at perhaps more flattering angles than our three-person selfies tend to turn out. Sofia hands Ella her phone, and the three of us pose in various contortions. Much as I try to smile my normal way, with the braces hidden behind my lips, we're making each other laugh so much that I almost forget to care. "You need to send those to us," I tell Sofia. "Don't be hoarding them all for yourself."

"I have to inspect them first and make sure I look cute," Sofia says, and Kensington and I smack her on her arms simultaneously. "Stop, I'm kidding!"

"You're not kidding, though, is the thing," Kensington says. "So listen, Vanity Queen of the Universe, are you ready to have your day made?"

"I was born ready," Sofia says.

"I propose that we go full-throttle tourist right now, and—"

"Times Square?!" Sofia asks.

"Absolutely not," Kensington says. "But Central Park does have a carousel, and it's pretty much the most vile, touristy thing you can do in the place."

"Let's go," I say. "I love a carousel."

"Who loves a carousel over the age of eight?" Kensington asks as we begin our descent.

"Everyone who wasn't born a crotchety old woman!" Sofia answers, linking her arm through mine and then Kensington's and dragging us along as she skips down the sidewalk.

"I don't skip!" Kensington calls.

"You do now!" Sofia tells her, and we do—all the way down a winding path leading into the heart of Central Park. We unlink ourselves only when we want to stop to take photos—motion-related or not—which happens approximately every five steps (followed by needing to immediately post our favorites on PhotoReady, which slows things down even more). Walking with Sofia through Central Park is like escorting a hyperactive puppy—everything excites her; everything, she swears, was once in a movie; and everything would make *such* a good picture. Her enthusiasm is contagious, even to Kensington, which means that it takes us at least three times longer to get around the park than it should.

We're in the midst of taking goofy pictures in front of Shakespeare's statue on Poet's Walk when I hear it— the faint sound of carousel music in the distance. "Are we close?" I stop posing to ask Kensington. "I hear a giant music box."

"You have the ears of a German shepherd," she tells me. "Yes, it's around the bend."

"Let's go!" Sofia says, and she takes off running down the tree-lined Mall.

"She's definitely going to get herself lost," Kensington

shakes her head as we start after her, Ella trailing farther behind. We reach Sofia when she's come to a stop at a fork in the path, and Kensington hurries in front of us. The music becomes louder and louder, and I rush to catch up with Kensington, linking one arm through hers and then reaching back my other for Sofia. We skip *Wizard of Oz*–style the rest of the way until the carousel appears before us.

"I'll get our tickets," I say. "My treat." I walk up to the booth and rustle in my bag for my wallet. "Three tickets, please," I request when I reach the window.

"Make that four," a voice calls over my shoulder. A male voice, so it can't be Ella, or Sofia, or Kensington. But it sounds almost as familiar.

I turn slowly to face the speaker, and there, right in front of me, is Tate. Tousled hair, emerald-eyed, perfect-smile Tate, there, as if a figment of my imagination.

I reach out and touch his shoulder, as if to make sure I'm not seeing things, which makes Tate laugh.

"I'm real, last I checked," he tells me. "How have you been, @AvalonByTheC?"

"What—I can't—where did you—" I stammer, before blurting out, "I have your scarf!" He tries to answer, but I continue blabbering. "But I don't have it with me—it's in our dorm room. But maybe you want to pick it up later, or I can mail it—" Before I can continue, Sofia and Kensington run up to us, saving me from my own jabbering.

"What are you doing here?" Kensington asks, shoving him playfully.

"What, did you think just because I got kicked out that I would go back to Boston with my tail between my legs?" he asks.

"But where have you been staying?" Sofia questions him. "Please don't tell me in that cardboard box I saw on the sidewalk outside Dingymist Dorm."

"My uncle lives in the city," Tate explains. "So I've been crashing with him."

"I can't believe we ran into you," I say. "What are the chances, in a city this big?"

"Well . . . ," he begins. "You didn't exactly run into me. I made a point of running into *you*. You guys have been pretty busy on PhotoReady today. Once I saw you were in Central Park, I knew you'd come to the carousel, so I staked it out."

"I don't know whether that's sweet or creepy,"

Kensington says. "I'm leaning toward creepy."

"But why did you know we'd come here?" I ask him. "I didn't even know there was a carousel in the park before Kensington told us."

"Please," Tate says, that sparkly smile spreading across his face. "It's such a girl thing to do. No offense— the carousel *is* pretty great. I knew even Kenz wouldn't be able to resist it."

"So, speaking of the carousel . . . are we riding it or not?" Sofia asks.

"Oh, right," I say. I had gotten so distracted by Tate's appearance that I had stepped away from the booth without completing my purchase. I shuffle back and buy four tickets, and we step up to board as the carousel comes to a halt. The operator slides the gate open, and we dart onto the platform. I choose a giant white horse, and Tate picks a tiny gray pony next to mine.

"I'm pretty sure those are meant for preschoolers." I laugh at him.

"Just my speed," he says, holding up his phone. "Let's take a picture of us being preschoolers before the ride starts." I lean my head toward his, and he snaps a selfie of the two of us on our respective stallions.

"You'll have to send that to me," I tell him. "Of course, that would require giving someone your phone number, which doesn't seem to be your forte."

"Put yours in," he says, handing me his phone. I type my number into his contacts and name myself @AvalonByTheC.

"Are you texting it to me now?" I ask as the ride jolts into motion.

"Eventually," he replies with that signature grin. As the carousel makes its way round and round the dome, I snap photos of Kensington in front of me, Sofia behind me, Tate next to me. I take pictures of the moving horses and the rotating platform for our #PhotoRetreatMotion tag, and I even photograph myself. The carousel ride comes to an end entirely too soon, and Tate begins to dismount his horse before it's at a complete stop. Rebellious, as usual.

"Good seeing you three," he says. He pats the head of my horse twice and then steps off the carousel's platform, moving toward the exit.

"Wait!" I call after him. "What about your scarf?"

"Enjoy it," he replies. "I'll get it back some other time." With that, he jogs out into the park and away from us once again. And after he's gone from view, I continue to stare in that direction, as if waiting for him to pop up out of nowhere once again.

"*What* was that?" I ask as Sofia, Kensington, and I mosey off our saddles and away from the carousel. "Did he really disappear again?"

"International man of mystery," Kensington says, now linking her arms through mine and Sofia's. "I don't think we'll ever figure that one out. But at least you got to see him."

"*And* he gave you his number," Sofia says. "I saw that."

"Actually, I gave him mine," I clarify. "I never got his. And I doubt I'll hear from him."

"You definitely will," Kensington says. "I bet he left his scarf with you on purpose—it was a full-on Cinderella move. That's his glass slipper."

"Oh, please," I say. "That's so not what happened."

"He made a point of finding you today," Sofia adds. "A *point* of it."

"Of finding *us*," I correct her.

"He barely spoke to *us*; he came for *you*," she says. "That has to mean something."

"But what?" I ask. "What does it mean?"

"It means he wanted to see you," Sofia says. "It at least means that."

"So, guys?" Ella comes up behind us. "I received a text from Roberto—they're changing the location of our dinner to a place in Midtown. We can probably walk there if you like, but we should get going shortly."

"Where is it?" Kensington asks her, a vague look of suspicion flashing across her face.

"Forty-Fourth between Broadway and Eighth," Ella answers her. "Right off of—"

"Noooooooooo," Kensington moans.

"What is it? What's wrong?" Sofia asks, looking from Ella to Kensington to me and back again.

"I'm no expert," I begin, "but I'm pretty sure the place we're going is in the heart of . . ."

"Times Square?!" Sofia calls out, and Ella and I nod as Kensington buries her face in her hands.

"Finally!" Sofia leaps down the path ahead of us, so giddy that I'm convinced she's about to do a cartwheel. "Come on, Kensington. Time to go to your favorite #HometownAttraction!" She takes off running as if she knows where she's going, and the three of us struggle to keep up. We make our way out of the park and then down Broadway, and with every block, the signs around us grow taller, brighter, more sparkly, until finally, we are nestled directly in the middle of Times Square, in the heart of New York, in the center of the world. We look up, Sofia's wide eyes reflecting the glitter all around us.

"I can't believe I almost didn't see this," Sofia says. "You can't deprive a tourist like me of Times Square!" I laugh as I pull out my phone to take a photo, but after a beat, I place it back in my pocket. Because no picture can properly capture how I feel in this moment; that's something only my memory is capable of.

CHAPTER 23

After Sofia got her fill of Times Square, and Kensington got her fill of complaining about Times Square, the entire retreat group was escorted back to Dingymist Dorm to begin packing for our noontime departure tomorrow. Kensington is beyond smug when, fifteen minutes later, save for her sheets and a few toiletries, she is finished, while Sofia and I have barely gotten our suitcases out of the closet.

"Seriously, what are we going to do with our mural?" Sofia asks. "We hardly got to enjoy it."

"Maybe, since Kensington's sitting there, staring at us"—I clear my throat loudly at her—"she'd agree to print some duplicate photos so we can each re-create the mural at home."

Kensington rolls her eyes at this, but instead of arguing, she holds out her hands to take our phones. While she systematically begins printing pictures, Sofia and I scramble about the room, trying to throw all our items into bags. As we work, we polish off the remaining snacks, more so we won't have to pack anything extra than because we're hungry—even Sofia.

"So you never heard from Tate, huh?" she asks, picking up his scarf from my bed and tossing it casually into my suitcase.

"No," I say with a shrug. "Whatever. He's a weirdo."

"You certainly took enough pictures of this weirdo on the carousel," Kensington says, looking up at me with one eyebrow raised.

"As a great photographer once said," I begin, "'I photograph what scares me. I photograph the things I scare.'" This makes Sofia burst out laughing and Kensington roll her eyes even higher than the first time.

"I don't know how I put up with you two clowns for a whole week," she says.

"Oh, you know you love us," Sofia says, crossing the

room and pretending to sit on Kensington's lap, placing her arms around her neck. I come up behind them and wrap one arm around Kensington's shoulders and the other around Sofia's.

"We should promise to go to the same college in five years," I tell them. "Then we can live together all over again."

"Room six-oh-nine, version two-point-oh," Sofia says. "Agree to this, or we're never releasing you," she tells Kensington.

"Agreed, agreed," she says. "Now leave me in peace if you want these pictures sometime this century!"

Sofia and I return to packing, and Kensington returns to printing, but the efficiency lasts only a few minutes before Kensington calls out, "Hey, did you guys see this?" She holds out her phone with a picture on the screen.

A picture of Tate and me. The selfie he took on the carousel.

"How did you get that?" I ask her. "Did he finally text it to me?"

"No," she says. "He posted it on PhotoReady. It looks like it's the first time he's ever posted a picture with people in it, so if I were you, I'd be honored."

"That's soooooo sweet," Sofia says.

"Okay, he's cute, I'll admit it," I say. "But why did I have to smile like that in the picture?"

"Smile like what?" Kensington asks.

"With my teeth," I explain. "The braces ruin the whole thing, especially when he has such a perfect smile. A perfecto smile. You know, perfecto? Like El—"

"No, no, no changing the subject," Kensington says. "Is this what that whole #IfYouJustSmile nonsense was about? Where you never actually showed your smile?"

"I guess," I tell her. "I mean, you guys have seen pictures of my sister—her smile is almost as good as Tate's. And mine is, well, it's not. It's metal and kind of crooked and—"

"More gratifying," Kensington interrupts me again.

"Right," Sofia says. "Because when we get you to smile—to *really* smile—we know that you mean it. It's like a point of pride. Plus, your smile is beautiful, the same as Tate's or Arden's."

"Oh, stop it," I say. "No lying. You know that's not true. I know that's not true. It was a pity compliment."

"Yeah, you're right," Kensington says. "But we're also right. Your smile's not perfect, but it's very you. It doesn't open up to everyone. Only to the inner circle."

"I assume that makes us the inner circle," Sofia says.

"Hey, you two can stop psychoanalyzing me now," I say. "You, get back to printing. You, get back to packing."

"You didn't answer me," Sofia says. "Are we or are we not the inner circle?"

"You are," I tell her. "You're practically the bull's-eye."

"Very good." Sofia nods with satisfaction. "But don't tell your other bull's-eye that."

"Who?" I ask.

"Celia, duh," Sofia answers.

"Yeah, if you two end up in another spat, we won't be there to fix the problem," Kensington quips, rolling her eyes yet again.

"You know, if you keep doing that, they're going to get stuck up there," I tell her. "At least, that's what my grandmother always told me."

"Let's focus on the happy news of the evening," Sofia says. "Tate's selfie with Avalon."

"Oh, for the love . . . Could we please talk about someone besides me?" I say, tossing a licorice stick at her.

"Fine, let's talk about me," Sofia says.

"Your favorite topic," Kensington remarks as all of a sudden, the twinkle lights go dark.

"Did you unplug those?" Sofia asks.

"No, Miss Accusatory," Kensington answers. "They went out on their own."

"We must have burned them out by keeping them on all the time," I reason. "It's a fitting end, really." And as much as I had wished—was it only a day ago?—for the end of the week to come sooner, for me to head home immediately, now that it was happening, I couldn't help but wish for just one more night in the infamous Room 609.

CHAPTER 24

The following morning, we have a truncated class with Roberto before we're released for a final photographic journey. Not only does Roberto have a "motion" photograph from each of the three of us in the collage for discussion today (carousel for me, fountain for Sofia, taxi for Kensington), but he also makes a point of complimenting each of them.

"I guess we're not on the blacklist anymore," Kensington whispers.

"Way to redeem ourselves at the last minute," I say, extending a palm to both of them for a silent high five.

"I assume you haven't checked PhotoReady yet," Sofia says to me quietly.

"Why, what did Tate do now?" I ask, but Sofia only shrugs a response. I quickly open the app, and as I scroll through my feed, I find picture after picture of . . . me. All of them taken this week, and posted by either Sofia or Kensington. Underneath each photo is a single label: #IfYouJustSmile. And sure enough, in every one, I'm smiling—sometimes a smirk, sometimes a full-on grin—and I must admit that while it's not a perfect smile, it *is* a happy one.

"Good thing you have such talented photographer friends, huh?" Sofia says proudly. "There are so many potential profile pictures in there."

"Yeah, you're welcome," Kensington says.

"They're great, really," I say. "I can't believe you took all these without me noticing."

"You were too busy trying not to smile that you didn't notice when you were," Sofia says. "Now what has Roberto been droning on about? I haven't been listening."

"Something about photographing reflections," Kensington answers. "Mirrors and water and that nonsense. Get it? Because we're 'reflecting' on our week." Kensington does one of her best eye rolls to accompany this statement.

"Shhhh." One of the other retreaters shushes us, but I don't feel my cheeks flush pink with embarrassment as they usually would. I'm too distracted by my phone buzzing with a text. *Rebels until the end*, Kensington writes. *Nice work, 609.*

Toward the end of my final hour with Kensington and Sofia, my phone begins vibrating with a multitude of texts. Every single one of them is from Arden with some variation of *We're heeeeeeeeeere* (the number of *E*s is accurate).

"My family's here," I tell my roommates, sounding sadder about it than I mean to.

"Boo," Sofia says. "I mean, sorry. I guess it's okay if you're excited to see them."

"I'm more excited to see my cat," I say. "The poor thing's been cooped up with the neighbor all week."

"I'm so glad I only learned now that you're a crazy cat lady," Kensington says. "If I had known this early on, no way I could have gotten past that."

"You're going to love it even more when you find out the cat's name," I tell her.

"I can't even bear to think . . . ," Kensington begins,

pretending to place her hands over her ears. "Don't tell me Whiskers or Fluffy or—"

"Jelly," I tell her. "Jelly Kelly."

"That is *adorable*!" Sofia exclaims.

"Best you stop now before I lose *all* respect for you," Kensington says. "Pretty soon you'll be telling me that you like scented candles, too."

"Hey, I love candles!" Sofia pipes up.

"Honestly, I don't know how I lived in the same space as you two for a week," Kensington says, shaking her head as my phone begins vibrating yet again. "Is the cat calling?" she asks, her favorite smirk plastered across her face.

"Very funny," I say. "But I guess I really do have to go find them. . . ."

"Which means it's almost time for me to get whisked away to the airport by Ella," Sofia says, pouting.

"I'm sure you'll find your journey to be perfecto," I tell her. "I assume you're taking yourself home?" I ask Kensington.

"Indeed," she says. "A straight shot up on the 1 train."

"Where do you live anyway?" Sofia asks.

"The Upper West Side," she answers.

"Wait, where we went the first night?" I ask. "You took us to your own neighborhood and didn't tell us?"

"Yep, we passed my apartment building too," Kensington says. "You know, you're not the only one who likes to be reminded of home every once in a while, Avalon Kelly."

Sofia's own phone starts ringing then, with Ella's name appearing across her screen. "I guess this is it, then," she says before answering. She does some silent nodding, says, "Okay," a few times, and then hangs up. "I have to meet her now."

"Where's your family?" Kensington asks me. "Are you walking to the dorm with us?"

"Arden says to meet them by the fountain in Washington Square Park," I say. "So . . ."

"Listen, no big sappy good-byes—let's go," Kensington says, holding out her arms for a three-way hug. "I'll talk to you goofballs later."

"I hate this," Sofia says. "I had the best week with you guys. It was the greatest first trip to New York in the history of the world."

"Remember our college plan," I remind them. "In five years, Room six-oh-nine will live on, forever in infamy."

We pull apart and stand there, none of us wanting to walk away first.

"One more picture?" Sofia suggests, and we all lean our heads together dutifully.

"Wait, I want to take one too," I say, and I snap a photo with my own camera.

"Last one," Kensington says, whipping out hers. Once we each have a picture, we move apart from one another, standing in silence. "Okay, enough of this. Avalon Kelly, get to your family. Short Stack, let's go collect your eighty-seven suitcases."

"Wait, then you two will have another good-bye without me," I whine as they walk away.

"Don't cry because it's over. Smile because it happened," Kensington calls over her shoulder with her typical smirk.

"Who's the cliché now?" I yell back to her. I watch them round the corner and then I take a deep breath, trying to prepare myself for my family's onslaught of questions. How could I ever answer them? And tell them how great and how terrible, how amazing yet unexpected the week truly was?

"Avalon!" I hear my name being called, and for a

minute, I think Sofia and Kensington must be returning. "Avalon!" Another voice this time.

I turn around and see Arden and my parents rushing toward me.

With Celia right beside them.

"What are you guys . . . ?" I begin, but Arden and Celia have descended and embraced me in a tight hug, both squeezing me hard. And even though this morning I hadn't necessarily been looking forward to seeing them, and even though I didn't want to leave all that Sofia and Kensington and I had created this week, I find that once they're back with me, I can't imagine how I ever left.

"What are you doing here?" I say quietly to Celia, in between greeting my parents. "I didn't know you were coming."

"Your parents asked me, so I thought I'd surprise you," Celia explains. "I hope that's okay."

"Of course it is," I say. "I'm sorry if I was a bad friend this—"

"You're the best friend," Celia says. "You're *my* best friend. I think I was afraid of losing you to your new best-friend roommates, and I freaked out."

"You didn't, and you won't," I assure her. "Now, what's

with all the bags?" They each have a large shoulder bag slung across their sides, and Dad is dragging a suitcase behind him.

"We decided to book two hotel rooms for the night," Mom tells me. "So that we have the whole rest of the day for you to take us to some of the places you've been this week. Arden was showing us the pictures you were posting."

"You created a PhotoReady account?" I ask her incredulously, as if this is the biggest surprise of my day.

"I caved," Arden says. "I couldn't bear the curiosity of what you were up to, since you were barely sending any news. But don't expect me to use it from now on."

"But where are we going to put my stuff from the dorm room?" I ask my parents. "We have to get it out today."

"The hotel is right down the street," Dad says. "We'll make a couple of trips if we have to. And then you can decide where to take us first."

I begin leading my family and Celia down the sidewalk, taking the Kensington–New York–expert position at the front of the pack. And though I had feared I wouldn't know how to tell them what I saw, what I learned, and what I loved this week, the memories pour out of me as we make our way through the city. These are my people—the ones who bring me to my comfort zone, and with whom I can most easily be myself. The ones who will share new experiences with me, and help me reflect upon the ones I've had without them. But if this week has shown me anything, it's that there are many people out there in the world—more than I ever thought possible—who can genuinely make me smile, this time with my full face, and all at once.

ACKNOWLEDGMENTS

Big Apples of thanks to Alyson Heller, whose Broadway marquee would read EDITOR EXTRAORDINAIRE!

Avenues of gratefulness to Charlie Olsen for being an agent as dazzling as Times Square!

Skyscrapers of appreciation to Mara Anastas, Fiona Simpson, Faye Bi, Kayley Hoffman, Jessica Handelman, Carolyn Swerdloff, and the rest of the Aladdin team for making books as merry as the Central Park carousel!

HERE'S A SNEAK PEEK AT THE NEXT
BOOK FROM ALLISON GUTKNECHT:
Sing Like Nobody's Listening

When I reach Jada's locker Monday morning, she is nowhere to be found. I lean against it, watching the bustle of the hallway move past me while pulling out my phone to text her.

Where are you?

I wait a minute, then two, with no response. This wasn't like Jada. She usually arrived at school before me, or at least at the same time. And if she was running late, she always told me, but I hadn't heard a peep from her since Saturday.

I wander down the seventh-grade wing, waving at Mrs. Nieska as I pass her door. I turn down the hallway toward the front of the school, where I spot Jada's long licorice locks ahead of me. Relieved, I start to approach until I see who she's standing with:

The theater people.

At least eight of them. Maybe twelve.

I walk past their circle quickly, half wanting Jada to see and run after me, and half hoping she doesn't notice me at all. I make a left to circle back to our homeroom, where I see Libby coming my way. And at the moment, I'm grateful to have someone—anyone—to talk to. As if to prove to myself that if Jada can make new friends, then I can too.

"Hi, Wylie!" Libby calls brightly, brushing the strands of her French braid back and forth over her fingers like a tiny broom. "Have a good weekend?"

"I did," I lie. "How about you?"

"It was okay," she answers as we reach each other. "I was trying to get ready for the fall musical auditions, but I kept getting distracted."

"You're auditioning for the musical?" I ask, trying to shield the surprise in my voice. Was *everyone* auditioning for the musical?

"Shocking, I know," Libby says, wrinkling the freckles on her nose. "My dad thinks it would be good for me to join a group to 'find my niche' in middle school." She forms her fingers into quotation marks as she says this.

"I figure, at the very least, maybe they'll need someone to help with sets. I'm hoping I could handle painting a backdrop blue. As long as they didn't want me to actually draw something. That'd put me back to the drawing board. Literally."

I smile at her. "Jada is auditioning too," I reveal.

"Jada's auditioning and you're not?" Libby asks. "But what if she gets a part?"

"What do you mean?" I ask, even though, in truth, I know exactly what Libby means. That Jada and I do everything together. And if she's in the musical, then what will I do?

"Hey, maybe you should audition too," Libby suggests, instead of answering my question. "That way, at least one person will be there for moral support when I look like a deer caught in headlights up there."

I shake my head. "I'm definitely not auditioning."

"Why not?" Libby asks. "It could be fun."

"Trust me, it wouldn't be," I tell her. "Not for me. I'm someone who's meant to be in the audience, not onstage."

"I don't believe that," Libby says. "I remember you and Jada doing the talent shows in elementary school.

I know you can sing a thousand times better than me."

At the mention of the talent shows, my toes curl in my shoes, as if they're trying to grip the floor more tightly. "I haven't sung in front of people since then," I say, not explaining the details as to why, and hoping Libby doesn't recall.

"Then it's time to rip off the bandage!" Libby says. "Do you want to come to my house later? We can prepare together. Or we can turn on the premiere of *Non-Instrumental*, and say we prepared."

"You watch that too?" I ask, but the morning bell rings before Libby can answer. "Here, give me your number and I'll text you." I hand her my phone, and as she plugs in her information, my thoughts swirl around like merging schools of fish. Maybe Libby's suggestion wasn't that crazy—maybe I *should* audition for the musical. The stage . . . thing—it *had* been more than three years ago. Maybe I should get over it, move on, put it behind me. Libby was right: prior to that talent show, I had enjoyed singing. I had even been okay with doing so in front of a crowd. Maybe it was time to try again.

Plus, if I auditioned, wouldn't that solve the Jada

problem? We could be in the musical together. I could become friends with the theater people too. I would have a group of friends of my own, *plus* my best friend. It could be ideal.

That is, of course, if I managed to stay on the stage.